A
LOCKDOWN
LOVE AFFAIR

KIRSTEN S. BLACKETER

A LOCKDOWN LOVE AFFAIR

Printed in the United States of America.
First Printing, 2020
ISBN: 978-1966905080

Written by Kirsten S. Blacketer.
Published by BlackShip Press
Kirsten.blacketer@gmail.com

https://kirstensblacketer.com

DEDICATION

My motto for 2020: Embrace the suck.

To Adam Driver, my inspiration for Ben.

To my husband and kids, who had to deal with me during lockdown in Italy. Here's to the memories.

To JK, I'm glad you got the joke.

A Letter from the Author

Dear Reader,

While the situation that sparked the idea for this story is real, the story itself is a work of fiction using details and tidbits from my observations during this global pandemic. This story provided an emotional outlet for me during two months of lockdown in Italy. It became my way of processing uncertainty and disappointment. Ben and Penelope's characters contain equal parts of me, which is why they make such a perfect couple. I hope you enjoy their love story.

This book is not a political statement. It is a work of romantic fiction aimed solely at showing the importance of human connection and understanding.

We all have unseen struggles we're dealing with, so let's be kind to one another.

With best wishes and love,

Kirsten S. Blacketer

P.S. Forgive any inaccuracies concerning Brooklyn. This country girl did the best she could with the research available. I had to make a few things up.

Thanks for understanding and enjoy.

Table of Contents

CHAPTER ONE
LOCKDOWN

BEN

LOCKDOWN DAY 1

Don't panic. It's not the end of the world. It only feels like it.

I grip the remote tighter instead of throwing it against the wall. I want to see it shatter, but the thought of cleaning up another mess leaves me desperate for some form of control. Damn it. I have plans. I have work to do. If they lock the city down, I'm done. I groan when the mayor steps up to the microphone and announces the fate of the city, at least for the foreseeable future.

Non-essential businesses are closed until further notice. City-wide lockdown. Stay at home. Self-quarantine.

The words hover in the air like a poisonous cloud threatening to choke me.

Damn it. I shoot to my feet and, this time, throw the remote. The satisfaction of impact is short-lived. Just like I knew it would be, and now I have to buy a new remote. One more fucking thing. Great. Just wonderful. I stalk to the TV and jerk the plug out of the wall. Unnecessary, yes. But it makes me feel better.

My phone pings in rapid succession as a flurry of texts come in. I rub my hands over my face. Why? Of all the times for a pandemic to hit, why now? Why couldn't it have hit after the merger? Now I'm stuck in my goddamn apartment, and I sure as hell can't finalize this deal from home. What if I need files from the office? Specific records? The things I need to do my job might as well be half a world away. We are so fucked.

I stare out the window at the Brooklyn skyline. The sun casts long shadows over the city as it sets. I catch a glimpse of the neighboring building whose rooftop is nearly level with my floor. Dying sunlight highlights the pots and raised garden beds occupying part of the roof. The small table and two chairs sit empty. I rack my brain. Were those there last week?

I shake my head. It doesn't matter. Normally, I'm not home to even notice anything outside my windows. This apartment is merely a place to crash when I'm not at the office.

My phone pings again. I have to deal with it sooner or later. The company needs direction, and with Evan out of town I need to be on my game. Lockdown or not, I'm still in charge. There're mountains of work to do until the merger is complete. I can't take the chance of anything going wrong.

I grab the phone. Fourteen messages. Half of them are from Evan. If I don't call him, he'll keep blowing up my phone. I hit the call button.

"Holy shit, you returned my call. Are you dying?" Evan sounds surprised.

"What do you want?" I pointedly ignore his snarky question.

"I saw the news." The unspoken implications pull tight like a rubber band.

I want to snap, but I grind my teeth instead. "I have it under control."

"I know. I'm not worried about the merger. I'm worried about you."

"Why?"

"Because you live at the office, Ben. Do you even have food at your apartment?"

My gaze drifts to the kitchen. Do I have anything here? "This is Brooklyn. I can get a pizza delivered at 3:00 am if I want it."

Evan grumbles under his breath. "Dickhead."

"You know I can hear you." I open my laptop and press a few keys, pulling up my inbox.

"Well, you are. Anyway, are you going to be okay working from home for a few days?"

"Yeah, I have some of the files here. Once things relax a little, I'll get back in the office and finalize the paperwork for Mr. Kennedy."

"I'll try to get back to the city as soon as I can."

"Why? There's nothing for you to do here but sit on your ass." I pause for effect. "Wait, you do that normally."

"You're a riot. No wonder you're still single."

"So are you. Or did you find the new love of your life in the Poconos?" I'm sick of lectures on my inability to connect with a woman from someone who finds his soulmate every time he travels.

"No." The waver in his voice betrays him.

"Bullshit."

"Fine. There might be someone, but it's nothing serious."

"Keep telling yourself that." I scan the inbox and find an email from Empire Industries. "Has Mr. Kennedy reached out to you since you left?"

"No. Why?"

I read the email aloud, and my heart sinks. Shit.

"He wants the financials on top of the proposals?" Evan whistles low. "Do you have access to that stuff from home?"

"Not all of it." Panic claws at the back of my throat. I force it down. "But that shouldn't matter."

"Do you need me to come back to the city?" Evan's reliable, but when it comes to this kind of stuff, he's more trouble than help.

"No, I've got it under control." I take a deep breath. "What day are you coming back?"

"Sunday night."

"Okay. Go enjoy your trip. I've got work to do."

"Don't overthink it, Ben."

I scoff. "Later."

Once I disconnect the call, I toss the phone aside and rake my hand through my hair.

"Shit." I glance at the pack of cigarettes sitting near the door by my keys. I'm dying for one. I've been trying to quit for weeks. This is a hell of a time to give them up.

I settle for a beer from the fridge, ignoring the absence of any real food in the refrigerator, and collapse on the couch. I scroll through the rest of the unread emails.

There is plenty of work to keep me busy. Just because I'm at home and not at the office doesn't mean I can't be productive. Besides, the lockdown can't last that long. This city has seen some shit. It's been through terrorist attacks and financial recessions. And if the past is anything to go by, New Yorkers are resilient and badass. There's no way a city of this size and fortitude will come to a screeching halt because of a global pandemic.

Even as I think it, dread settles like a dark cloud over my head.

PENELOPE

LOCKDOWN DAY 1

I set the last few items in the box and close the lid. There. That should do it. I nod approvingly at the stack of boxes littering the hallway. Finally. It took me four months to sort through all of my grandparents' possessions. After they both passed away in November, I found every excuse to avoid going through their belongings. It hurt too much every time I opened a door, only to find the room filled with empty reminders. They meant everything to me, and now they're gone.

Sadness settles around me for a moment. "I miss you both so much." My hand slides over the box. As the eldest granddaughter, I had the strongest bond with them. Nearly every summer and holiday meant a trip to the city to stay with Grandma and Grandpa. So many memories lay within this historic brownstone. I cried when the lawyer told me I'd inherited it. I'd never thought I'd find myself living in Brooklyn, especially in a world without my grandparents. When I moved in, the small reminders of them became overwhelming. After a few months, I found it easier to deal with their estate than to drown in it. It helped me process the overwhelming loss. Still, I miss them desperately, but at least they're together and at peace.

A week before my trip to visit them for Thanksgiving, they died in a horrible car accident. I should have been here, but I wasn't. Nothing can change that ache in my heart telling me I could have done something to prevent it.

No, I will not dwell on it. Not today. I can't change the past with regrets and wishful thinking. I glance around the house and see how much I've accomplished. It needed to be done. So I did it, for them and for me.

Now, if I could just find the motivation to haul this stuff to the empty basement apartment Grandpa used for storage.

I grab my keys and open the front door. It'll take a few trips, but I think I can manage it tonight.

Ooof. I collide with someone on my front doorstep. "Oh, my goodness, I'm so sorry." I straighten quickly.

"Quite alright, Miss Weiss." My grandparents' neighbor, Mr. Donovan, smiles at me before offering a piece of paper. He's in his sixties and normally looks quite spry. Today, exhaustion lines his face. "I take it you've seen the news?"

I stare at him puzzled. "What news?"

His gray brows furrow. "The mayor just announced a city-wide lockdown."

I blink at him, confused. "Lockdown?"

"Yes. You cannot leave your home unless it's for a medical emergency or to purchase necessary supplies. All non-essential businesses are required to close." His eyes widen behind his bifocals. "I've never seen anything like it in all my years."

"Wow." I glance at the paper in my hand. A notice from the city with instructions and contact information. "Thank you."

"Where are you going?"

"I have to take some things to the basement and then run to the market for dinner." I gasp. "Am I still allowed to do that?"

"It should be fine." He nods. "But tomorrow, I would advise staying home if you can. This virus is nothing to sneeze at." He chuckles at his own pun.

"Am I able to tend my garden on the roof at least?" I ask, tucking the paper into my pocket.

He nods after a moment of thought. "I don't see a problem with that. It's your roof. Not like you're wandering around the city aimlessly." He winks. "I'm looking forward to some of those fresh herbs and vegetables you promised me."

"Of course." A wave of relief washes over me. At least I have my garden. "They've already started sprouting. It's sure to be a bountiful harvest."

He smiles. "I hope so. If you need anything, please, don't hesitate to call me."

"I will." I wave as he walks down the steps. "Thank you."

Over the next hour, I transfer the boxes from the house upstairs to the basement apartment. Grandpa had converted the basement of the brownstone into a separate apartment in the hope I would come live in the city permanently. I wish I had taken him up on the offer after I graduated college. Regrets only serve as a hurdle, and I am determined to move forward. When I finally collapse on the couch, it's completely dark outside.

Damn. I wanted to check on the garden. It will have to wait until morning. I shower and run to the corner market to pick up some items for dinner as well as supplies for the week. Once I'm back home, I make some dinner before flopping in front of the television. I ignore cable completely and turn on Netflix. They just released the new season of the science fiction show I love.

After my grandparents' accident, I moved to the city to execute their will. Their estate covers my expenses, so there's no rush to find a job. Not that I've thought about it until now. Am I even going to stay in the city? It's not like I have anything keeping me here. Still, it would be an adventure, living the city life after growing up in rural Pennsylvania. Maybe I'll take some time and see what Brooklyn has to offer me.

Even if the city wasn't on lockdown, I would have never noticed. The market was busier than usual, but that tended to happen in the evenings. It took me a few months to acclimate to life in the city. I may never get used to the hustle of city living, although it is exciting.

I have a gorgeous home, a promising rooftop garden, and financial stability. What more could a girl possibly ask for?

I settle on the couch and snuggle beneath my favorite afghan. The show starts, and I'm drawn into the new season. I wish Lucy were here to watch it with me. I reach for the phone to call her and hang up when she doesn't answer. Damn, she must be working second shift at the hospital this week.

Then I remember the lockdown and the pandemic. I hope she's okay. I make a mental note to call her in the morning and then lose myself in the show.

CHAPTER TWO
THE LADY IN RED

BEN

LOCKDOWN DAY 2

I want to throw my laptop out the window. None of the numbers make sense. I sent an email to my creative team before I went to sleep, and only half of them responded. I shove my phone into my back pocket and stalk into the kitchen.

Even though the caffeine is making me twitchy, I pour my third cup of imported coffee. Does my hand always shake like this? I hold it up and try to keep it still. It wobbles. Not enough to be noticeable, but enough to make me feel uncomfortable.

Maybe it isn't the coffee. It could be stress. Yeah, it's the stress. Has to be. Between the citywide lockdown and the inability to gather the paperwork I need to ensure this merger, I'm stuck. The walls seem closer together. Is this room smaller? I can't breathe.

I shove away from the table and stalk down the hallway to my bedroom. I cross to the far window and open it. A cool breeze drifts through. It must be after noon because the sun has shifted behind the building and out of view.

I slip out onto the fire escape. I haven't been out here since I moved in, but I'm desperate for some fresh air. Of its own accord, my hand reaches for the pack of cigarettes in my robe pocket. I smoked one before I went to bed.

Nine. There are nine left in the pack. I can make them last. I don't need them. I drape my arms over the metal railing and hang my head. What the hell have I become? It's only been a day stuck at home and I feel like I'm falling apart.

Several deep breaths later and my heart slows. It's quiet, more than normal. The typical bustle of the city with the congested traffic, blaring horns, and endless chatter…it's dimmed. I stare out over what little piece of the city my side of the building overlooks.

She's still, almost peaceful. That can't be right. The city that never sleeps takes a well-earned nap. Weird. I've never heard it so quiet. A shiver of unease snakes through me. This whole thing is strange in a way I don't want to examine too closely. Besides, it's not like I have anyone in my life other than Evan to discuss it with, so I shove it into a mental box and hide it in the dark reaches of my mind, hoping it'll disappear.

I ignore the urge to run inside and turn on the television. But I know how the media works, and I don't have the patience to wade through speculation to find a nugget of truth. I've avoided it so far. I deleted all the social media apps from my phone too. I don't want to know. The anxiety of not being in control kills me.

I need to stay on task. Work. The merger. Focus. I have plenty to keep me occupied. Maybe I should set up a group meeting via VidBoom to ensure the team is keeping up with their work while we're out of the office.

Fuck, when did I become that guy? The fucking workaholic with no friends who can't turn it off. I rake my hand through my hair.

"Damn it."

A creak echoes across the alley. I glance around, expecting one of my neighbors to poke their heads out one of the windows. Nothing.

Then I see it. A flicker of movement on the rooftop opposite me. Flashes of red and tan blink against the sunlight. A woman rounds the corner carrying a bag. She's wearing a red sundress and a floppy brimmed hat. I shake my head. Some old lady trying to tame the city with a rooftop garden.

Good for her.

My phone rings. The sound makes my heart jump in my chest. I pull it out and answer, turning my back to the rooftop garden.

"What's up?"

It's work. Good. I need a distraction.

"Hold on, would ya? I have to get my charts out."

I dip back inside the window and close it. The woman in the garden is watching me. She waves.

She's not old. I can see that now, not in detail, but enough to put her close to my own age. Shit.

I ignore the pull of curiosity and retreat to the kitchen. Once there, I push the speakerphone button and open my files. "Let's go over the last year then."

My gaze drifts to the window and the pop of red in the corner of my vision. Don't be a fucking creep. This isn't social hour. Focus. There's work to do.

PENELOPE

LOCKDOWN DAY 2

An unfamiliar ringtone echoes behind me. I jump and spin around, looking for the noise.

A man scrambles to his feet on the fire escape that crisscrosses the building across the alley. I barely catch a good look at him before he ducks through the window back into the seventh-floor apartment, nearly dropping the phone in his hand as he does so.

I giggle at the absurdity of it all. He acts like being caught outside is a crime. I shake my head. The city might be in lockdown, but it's not like it's illegal to step outside to get some fresh air.

I get notifications when there's an update on the city's pandemic response, but otherwise, I keep the news off. A steady diet of that crap will rot my brain, since most of it is speculation and projection anyway. Life's too short to worry about things I can't control.

When he looks up, I wave. We all need a little bit of comradery during these crazy times. Even me. I've only been in the city for a few months, but I've made a handful of friends. It's nice to have some local connections.

Life here is so much different than growing up in small-town Pennsylvania. My grandparents might have left me all their worldly possessions, including a posh brownstone in Brooklyn Heights and a cozy bank account, but I'd trade it all to get one more day with them. I shake the thoughts from my mind and turn back to the garden.

The man across the alley doesn't seem interested in being friendly. Oh well. I set back to work on the raised garden beds draped with protective sheets to encourage germination. The seedlings should be ready for daily exposure soon, and they'll need complementary flowers to draw pollinators. I make a mental note to put that order in with the garden center before retrieving the pots from the shed on the roof.

My grandmother started this garden years ago, much to Grandpa's frustration. He built the shed for her to store the supplies for easy access and to save himself multiple trips to the basement every year. A country girl at heart, Grandma maintained a garden up until the day she died. It was her pride and joy. Now, it will be mine.

Never did I imagine I'd trade my job as a high school English teacher for a life of gardening leisure in Brooklyn. When I came here, I expected to want to return to my life in rural Pennsylvania. I'm not much of a city girl, honestly. But after meeting Lucy and inheriting the estate, I realized I could take this opportunity to find a new path in life, explore all the options. Unfortunately, lockdown is determined to delay my new adventure. Oh well, I'll just enjoy the journey one day at a time until things level out.

I turn on some music and work until the sun sets over the horizon. The city lights flicker in the distance. I stop and stare out at the Manhattan skyline beyond the treetops in the distance. So beautiful. I sigh and gather my things.

The lights in the building across the alley catch my attention. The woman on the sixth floor is working out in her living room. The gentleman on the eighth floor is pacing from one room, through to the next, and back again, while he talks on the phone. The seventh floor is dark except for one window where a shadowed outline stands.

The man from the fire escape earlier. I cannot see his face, but I know he's watching me. I can feel his gaze, and I shiver. I glance up at the dim lamp over my head. He knows I see him too.

When I turn back, he's gone. Curiosity nags at the back of my mind. I shrug it off and retreat into the building.

My phone rings as soon as I close the rooftop door. LUCY flashes across the screen, and I accept the call.

"Hey, I thought you were working second shift?"

"I am. I'm on break right now. How are you holding up?" Lucy's the closest thing I have to a best friend in the city. She works as an ER nurse at the Brooklyn Hospital Center, which is how we met. She'd been the nurse who'd delivered my grandparents' personal items to me. A friendship took root instantly.

"I'm fine. How are you?"

"Don't deflect. Seriously. How are you doing? Do I need to come check on you?"

"Lucy, you know better than anyone we're supposed to be practicing social distancing. Plus, I don't want you wasting whatever free time you have checking on me."

"Who else is going to check on you?" She pauses, but before I reply, she interjects, "And the old guy next door doesn't count."

"Mr. Donovan checks on me every day. I'm fine. Really. How's the hospital?"

"Busy. Lots of cases coming through. Still waiting on results to see if it's this damn virus or just the flu making its rounds." She sighs. "I don't wanna talk about it. Distract me.

Just for a little while."

I laugh. "Okay, well, I found a huge box of cotton fabric when I was cleaning out the closets. I think I might try to make a dress or two. Want one?"

"You know how to sew?"

"Of course, Grandma taught me."

Lucy laughs. "No, I don't really do dresses, but thank you. At least I know you have something to keep you occupied during this mess."

"Oh, and get this. I was working on the roof today, and I think I have a stalker."

"What the hell?" Lucy screeches into the phone like a pterodactyl. "Did you call the cops?"

"Calm down." I soothe her by explaining the details of the afternoon's adventure. "See. It's fine. I just thought it was funny. That's all."

"This city is full of freaks and pervs, Penelope. I was raised here. Don't take any shit from them, you hear me?"

"Yes, Mom." I roll my eyes and grab a drink from the fridge. "I didn't get a good look at him. But those apartments in that building are insanely expensive."

"Pervs come in all sizes, Girl. Money just makes them harder to prosecute."

I nod, even though I know she can't see me. She's not wrong, but I have a gut feeling about the fire escape guy. "He didn't feel like a perv. Just…lonely. I dunno." I shake my head.

"Girl, these are crazy times. And crazy times make people even crazier than normal. Just promise me you'll be safe. I can send Joey over to check on you."

I laugh. "Okay. I promise. Just don't send your brother to check on me. Please. I don't need some hulking Italian intimidating everyone within a five-block radius, okay?"

"Alright. Fine. But you call me if that creep tries anything pervy, got it?"

"Yeah. I'll keep you posted."

"Shit. I gotta go. Someone just coded. Love ya." The call

disconnects before I can reply.

"Love you, too, Lucy." I toss the phone aside and stumble toward the shower with my beer. I just can't shake the suspicion that I'm not the only one who's spending this lockdown alone.

Chapter Three
A New Bad Habit

Ben

Lockdown Day 7

I sit by the open window in the kitchen. It's another gorgeous spring day in the Heights and that only irritates me more. I turn my attention back to the spreadsheets in front of me, but the cool breeze and sunshine are like a siren song for someone who hasn't run in a week. Annoyed, I push away from the laptop and stomp into the kitchen. Petty and childish, yes. But I'm about to go insane if I stay locked up much longer.

I don't have any excuse to go out. I don't have a dog to walk or an essential job. No, I'm trapped. I need to go to the office, but I don't want to run the risk of getting stopped by the cops and fined. It's not that I can't afford it. Truth is, I can't run the risk of anything casting a shadow over this merger. Call it superstition or whatever. This deal has to happen, or I might as well give Evan my notice now.

The trash is overflowing. I should take it out. Maybe that will help ease the restlessness. I gather the take-out containers and stuff them deep in the garbage bag before tying it off. I never realized before how much take out I consume. It's embarrassing really. Since I normally ate at work, I never saw the aftermath of my eating habits piled in the trash. Chinese, pizza, sushi, kebabs...I hang my head. Normally, I don't worry about it since my morning run burns it off.

Only, I haven't been running. It's been a week since the city went into full lockdown, and I'm already feeling the constraints on my mind and my waist. Maybe I should pull out those weights from under the bed and do some reps. Something to get the blood moving again.

I grumble under my breath as I slip on my shoes and put my key in my pocket. Out in the hallway, I breathe easier. At least it's a change of scenery. I reach the trash chute, only to find it taped off.

"Great."

I should be happy. This gives me an excuse to exercise. Seven flights of stairs between me and the dumpster. Going down is easy and it feels good to get my legs working again.

I toss the trash in the huge dumpster out in the alley before retreating into the building. Not a soul in sight. It's like the damn apocalypse or something. Part of me is relieved at the absence of people. Social interaction hasn't been a hardship during this lockdown since I prefer to be alone.

I wonder how bad it really is? I haven't checked the news. I tried once, but it twisted the anxiety already lodged in my chest. It's better if I remain focused on my business.

I need to get back to work, but I can only do so much from home. If this shutdown lasts longer than a month, everything I've built will disintegrate. The financial hit is bad enough. Don't even get me started on the stock market. Fuck.

As I climb the stairs, I welcome the exertion. It burns the anxiety from my mind until I reach my apartment. Inside, my phone is ringing. I fumble with the keys and open the lock just in time for the phone to go silent.

"Damn it." I snatch the phone from the table and unlock it. Three missed calls. Two from Andrew, my assistant, and one from…shit. "Mr. Kennedy."

The last person I wanted to hear from today. My finger hovers over the green button. I should call him back.

I press the button.

"Mr. Kennedy. Empire Industries." I blank for a moment. I expected his secretary. He always routes his calls through her. Then I remember the extenuating circumstances.

"Yes, this is Mr. Statler with Solus Incorporated. I'm sorry I missed your call. I was taking care of…something."

"Not to worry, Statler. I wanted to connect with you directly about the upcoming merger."

"Yes, sir. I will have the documents finalized by the end of next week and couriered to you directly."

"I see this shutdown hasn't hampered your work ethic, Statler. Good. This whole lockdown has us in a bind, especially with the social distancing orders and business restrictions. Perhaps it would be wise for us to postpone the meeting scheduled for April 17th until the beginning of May."

My heart seizes. He didn't cancel the meeting. The merger is still on. Breathe. "Of course, sir, that is the wisest course of action, considering the circumstances of the city."

"I'll have my secretary change the meeting and email you the new details. In the meantime, we'll continue forward with the process and adjust as necessary should the need arise."

"Agreed. Please don't hesitate to contact me if you have any questions or concerns in the meantime."

"I will. Enjoy working from home, Statler."

"You too, sir." I mumble a hasty farewell and end the call.

I can't stop my heart from racing. I lean against the table, bracing my hands on the edge to give me some stability. Breathe. It's not the end of the world. It's insanely difficult to quell the anxiety creeping into my mind. On a normal day, I could go for a run or bury myself in endless meetings to stave off the panic. But life isn't normal right now. I'm home. Alone. Trapped. My skin is crawling. Maybe I should do some push-ups or something. Damn.

The breeze drifts in through the window along with the faint strains of music. Is that Queen? I push away from the table. As I approach the window, I see the garden and the small shack sitting on the neighboring building's rooftop. She's back.

I lean against the frame and watch her work. She's sitting at the table with a variety of terracotta pots stacked beside it.

What is she doing?

She pulls a box from the shed and shuffles through it. Doesn't she work? I mean. I know not everyone is a workaholic, but is this a long-time personal hobby or just something to pass the time during lockdown?

The more I watch her, the more curious I become. I laugh and shake my head when she dances around the rooftop, pumping her fists in the air along to the music. It's the first time I've laughed in weeks.

She clips her long brown hair up into a messy bun before sitting down at the table. I'm sucked into her vibrant world. Her head bobs to the beat as she sets a pot on the table. She lays out paint and brushes before setting to work on her canvas.

I can barely make out her face from this distance. She's wearing a pair of torn jeans that hug her curves and an oversized sweatshirt, baring her skin as it slopes off her left shoulder. Just a glimpse of her lightens the pressure of anxiety suffocating my sanity. I haven't seen her on the roof for the past few days. I didn't realize until now how much I miss these little glimpses of her. Somehow, she's become a spot of sunshine in my dark world. I smile as she spins, using the small shovel as a microphone. At least one of us is handling the lockdown with grace.

I jerk away from the window. What the hell am I doing? Unease settles over me. Have I become some creep spying on my neighbor? I hazard one last glance before I turn away from temptation.

Is she looking at me?

With a shake of my head, I retreat into the kitchen. I don't know her, and she doesn't know me. Lockdown will ensure it remains that way. When I look in the refrigerator, I see something more distressing. A door full of condiments isn't going to be enough if I'm going to cut back on take-out.

I have to go shopping. Shit. I need a cigarette.

This is a hell of a time to quit smoking.

Penelope

Lockdown Day 7

The sunshine on my face is a warm, soothing caress. I know now why Grandma spent so much time on the roof in her garden. It truly is the most relaxing spot in the city. Even with the commotion around me, there is a sense of serenity up on the roof.

I tap my feet along to the music as I paint. I have a few dozen playlists, but this one is on repeat a lot lately. A bit of classic rock, some contemporary jams, and a handful of early 2000s hits keep me motivated.

My attention keeps drifting to the apartment on the seventh floor of the building across the alley. He's watching me again. While it's not a wholly comfortable sensation, I confess a zing of excitement at the thought of my shy neighbor's presence. I'm weird, I know, but I can't help it. Curiosity and all that.

When I look again, he's gone. The thrill turns to disappointment. I should say something to him. But how? It seems a bit silly, the two of us playing this game. I turn back to my project and lose myself in the artistic process.

Grandma wasn't a painter. She sewed when the weather wasn't good for gardening. I thought about taking a stab at some patterns I found in her small sewing room. But the weather's too nice to be inside today.

The faint aroma of cigarette smoke drifts past me. I spin around, expecting to see Mr. Donovan smoking on the neighboring rooftop. He checks on the progress of the gardens every couple of days. But it's not Mr. Donovan. I squint against the sun and scan the area.

It's him. The seventh-floor stalker. I shake my head. He's standing on the fire escape in a halo of smoke. His back is toward me, and I wonder if he knows I'm aware of his presence. He's tall. Wow. I hadn't realized just how tall he is.

Hard to tell exactly, but using the window frame as a reference, I'd put him at just over six feet.

Broad shoulders fill out his faded blue t-shirt. He's got a runner's build with defined arms. I tap the end of my paintbrush against my lips. Hot damn. His dark hair is overgrown, brushing his shoulders in places. As I watch him, he turns to face me, pushing his free hand through his hair. I wish I could see his face clearly, but I would definitely recognize him on the street if I saw him.

We both freeze when our eyes meet. I don't want to breathe. I'm afraid it'll scare him off. I lift my paintbrush and wave. I smile, even though I'm pretty sure he can't see it. He lifts the cigarette to his lips and takes a drag. As he lowers it, he waves in return, his face clouded by the smoke curling from his lips.

Well then. Contact made. I can't help but grin. At this moment, I realize just how lonely the past week has been. I barely notice in the moment, but connections like this give me joy. Is he lonely too?

I haven't noticed any other motion in his apartment aside from him, so he's not married. Perhaps his girlfriend doesn't live with him. A man in such a swanky apartment cannot be single. Not unless there's something seriously wrong with him.

I gasp and then giggle. Maybe Lucy's right? He's a creepy perv!

With a shake of my head, I turn back to my artistic masterpiece. He's still there, smoking and watching, while he leans against the brick wall in the shade. I try to ignore him, but his presence sends my brain into overdrive. I lick my lips and reach for my water bottle.

My phone rings, and I nearly spill water down my shirt. Why am I so jumpy? I grab the phone and take note of the caller. *Speak of the devil.* I hit the accept button.

"Hey, Lucy."

"Hey, sunshine. You sound like you're in a good mood."

"I am. Just painting on the roof. It's a gorgeous day."

"Uh-huh. Any sign of your stalker lately?"

I glance over at the fire escape. He's stubbing out the cigarette and ducking through the window. I pout. "Yeah, he was out smoking on the fire escape. He just went inside."

"Girl, I'm telling you. He's a perv. If he tries anything weird, like flashing you or whatever, call the cops. You don't have to deal with that shit."

"Oh my god, Lucy. He's not a perv. He just waved to me. I'm sure he's harmless." I suddenly doubt the sincerity of my statement. Perv? No. Harmless…most definitely not, especially where my hormones are concerned. I haven't seen him up close, but after marking his height and build, my mind fills in the blanks. The fantasy is so vivid it's almost unhealthy.

"But have you spoken to him? I mean, have you actually looked into his eyes? That's how you know. Eye contact is crucial in judging a man's character."

"You're jaded. Just because you think all men are sneaky bastards, doesn't make it true, Lucy." I sip my water.

"There may be some good men out there, but I haven't seen them hanging out in Brooklyn, I'll tell you that."

I shake my head. It's no use arguing with her. "What's up? Aren't you working today?"

"My shift starts at seven. I'm working nights for a while. Figure I can't do much else during the day but sleep anyway, right?"

"True."

"Could you do me a huge favor? We're running low on masks at the hospital. Would you make some fabric mask covers?"

I think for a moment. Grandma has a whole tote of cotton fabric in the closet. "Yeah, I can do that. Send me the style you want and I'll get started tonight."

"You're an absolute sweetheart. I owe you. I'd make them myself, but I don't know shit about sewing."

"Hey, it's the least I can do. I'm not working right now so it'll be good for me to dedicate my time to something useful."

"Plus, it'll keep you off the roof and away from the pervy neighbor."

"There's no convincing you otherwise, is there?"

"You country girls are so trusting." She laughs. "Do you need anything?"

"No. I'm going to go grocery shopping later. I'm good. Thanks."

"Okay. Stay out of trouble, will ya?"

I laugh. "You too. Later." I hang up the phone and set it aside. The sun's sinking on the horizon. I guess I should call it an afternoon if I'm going to start on those masks.

Within ten minutes, I have everything put away and organized. The weather channel said it might rain next week, which is fine. I have plenty to keep me busy.

Before I go inside, I glance at the seventh-floor apartment hoping for another glimpse of the tall, mysterious stranger. Yeah, my mind is definitely preoccupied.

CHAPTER FOUR
PHYSICALLY DISTANT, SOCIALLY CONNECTED

BEN

LOCKDOWN DAY 8

This is ridiculous. As I stand in line, I shift my weight from one foot to the other. I can finally see the front door of the bodega. The nearest one to my apartment is two blocks away. I'm terrified of what awaits me inside. An older couple, standing exactly six feet behind me, discusses the city-wide shortage of supplies in all the supermarkets and bodegas. I stare at the red mark on the sidewalk that reminds us to maintain our social distance.

I snort and cross my arms. If there was a contest for social distancing, I would take first prize. Let's just say I wasn't a fan of people before this whole mess. It is kind of nice to not have everyone crowding me for once. Personal space in the city is a paradox.

Five minutes pass. I've been standing in line for nearly an hour already, and my phone battery is almost dead. I should have stayed home. Take-out can't be that bad. Maybe I can order my groceries online and have them delivered. I make a note to check that option out as soon as I get home.

Everyone avoids eye contact. I mean, it's typical for people in the city to avoid you. Everyone does their thing and gets on with life. But this is somehow worse. People sidestep around me, giving me a wide berth. They barely glance at me, afraid I'll contaminate them with a single look. The ones who do meet my gaze stare at me in horror like I'm infected with the plague. I'm not sure which is worse: mandatory isolation at home or being watched with open suspicion.

I stick my hands in my pockets. The couple behind me has been talking nonstop since we got in line. I've heard more about the current situation from them than I have from the news since this whole pandemic began. Though, I don't know if I can believe half of it. I'm going to have to do some research when I get home. With so much information floating around, the perpetuation of misinformation is expected, if not commonplace.

My nose itches. The high pollen count in the spring air tickles the back of my throat. I made the mistake of coughing when I first got in line. I swear I felt the death stares as their heads pivoted in unison, searching for the source of the sound.

I never thought I would crave the non-judgmental isolation of my apartment. But here I am.

The line moves forward, and I advance to the next marker on the sidewalk. I'm making mental notes of the employees I need to call when I get home. I should check on my parents, but Indiana feels like a whole universe away right now. I wonder if they're in lockdown as well. I wouldn't know, because I haven't called them. Guilt hits me square in the chest.

The huge glass pane to my right glints in the sunlight. I glance at my reflection for a moment before I'm distracted by movement inside the market. Several people crisscross the available floor inside the shop, without invading the others' space like chess pieces moving on a life-size board. It's almost comical in a sad way. How have we gotten to this point?

The thought disintegrates in my head when I see her. The rooftop gardener. She's wearing dark jeans and a cream-colored jacket. Her hair lays in curls over her shoulder, swaying as she reaches for a box on the top shelf. It's just out of reach, but she rises on her tiptoes and grabs it.

The breath whooshes from my lungs. She's gorgeous. I had a gut feeling when I saw her painting yesterday, but the imaginary version of her I had built in my mind is nothing compared with reality. The smile on her lips when she retrieves the box successfully has me reeling. She tucks the box into her basket and moves away from the window, disappearing into the back of the store.

The hour I spent standing in line was worth it, if for this moment alone. This glimpse of her. I searched through the glass, hoping for another opportunity.

The line moves again, and I'm one step closer to being inside the market. There are three people ahead of me. I lick my lips. Will I be able to see her? The possibility makes me dizzy with anticipation.

Another five minutes pass. I'm just outside the door. I'm the next customer. I know she's still inside because I've been watching the only exit. My heart aches with disappointment at the possibility of missing my chance to see her up close.

My phone dings in my back pocket. I pull it out and glance at the text. It's Andrew. Work can wait until I get home.

"Excuse me. Can you please move?"

I glance up. She's right in front of me, her arms overflowing with grocery bags. Her kind hazel eyes skim over me for a second before a brilliant smile blooms across her lips.

"Oh." I must have drifted in front of the door. I step aside. "Sorry." My mumbled apology lodges in my throat and swells.

"Thanks!" This woman is a ray of sunshine. Blinding and vibrant. Energizing. The moment pops like a bubble when she walks away, her hips swaying with the weight of the groceries in her arms.

I stare after her, dumbstruck. I want to put my head through the glass window. How dense can I be?

"Son, it's your turn." The older gentleman behind me shouts to get my attention.

I shake off this strange feeling and go inside the grocery store. It's not until I'm home putting my purchases away that

I realize something.

We were closer than six feet, and she didn't look at me like I had the plague. Far from it.

A small seed of hope takes root in my soul, and for the first time since lockdown started, I find myself wanting something more than an existence dedicated to work.

PENELOPE

LOCKDOWN DAY 8

My arms ache by the time I reach my front door. I have to set them all down so I can unlock the door, but as I do so, they spill across the front step. Damn.

But I'm not upset. Not in the slightest. Because I saw him. At least I'm almost positive it was him. My stalker from the seventh-floor apartment. Okay, stalker might be a bit harsh. That's what Lucy calls him, but, oh sweet heavens, he's gorgeous.

I collapse in a chair after putting my cold items away. There's no way in hell he's single. No freaking way.

When I walked out of the shop, I was so irritated at the man blocking my path. He seemed sincere in his mumbled apology. But I couldn't hear a thing. I disappeared in those bourbon brown eyes. So soulful. So intense. I fan myself at the memory. I could've drowned in those eyes, drunk to high heaven and blissful beyond measure. Oh my god, since when have I ever been a poet or a romantic? I'm an optimist by nature, yes, but when it comes to relationships, I'm a realist. If it seems too good to be true, it probably is.

I chew on my fingernail. What in the world is wrong with me? I'm never this discombobulated over a man. Ever.

He's so tall. I was right. Just over six feet. Lord, I would climb him like a tree. I press my hand to my open mouth. What am I thinking? This is insane. I haven't even spoken to the man.

I remember his smell. The spicy bite of aftershave and soap. There was an undercurrent to it, a hint of something forbidden and consuming, like dark chocolate and cayenne pepper. What the hell is wrong with me? I'm never this...obsessive. Ever. I appreciate a handsome man, especially one that smells good, but this is a whole other level.

With a grunt, I push the thoughts away and focus on putting the groceries in the cupboard. Ten minutes later, curiosity overwhelms my common sense. I run to the cabinet in the hallway and get Grandpa's binoculars. Without making a noise, I amble toward the rooftop. I need to check on my plants, nothing conspicuous about that, right?

When I step onto the roof, the sun is just starting to dip below the western horizon. Long shadows lay across the rooftop. I step into the protective cover of the shed and lift the binoculars.

The light is on in his apartment. He's home. I see the shadows shift past the window, but I can't get a clear view. Damn it. This is so stupid.

But I'm desperate. I want to see him again. I want to study his face. I only caught a brief glimpse. He's handsome, but certainly not by any traditional standard. His long face seemed out of proportion, but still perfectly balanced with his full lips and mesmerizing eyes. Dark, wavy hair emphasized his pale skin peppered with imperfect freckles, and a thin, dark goatee framed his mouth. If I could put him in a movie, I'd cast him as the villain, if only by looks alone. This man was unlike any I'd ever met. Is he handsome? Is my mind playing tricks on me? I've never been so conflicted in my attraction to someone in my life.

But I want to see him again. I want to see him smile. I want to hear his laugh, his voice. The two words he muttered were nearly incoherent. I stomp my foot with impatience. Was I really fantasizing about some stranger? I drop the binoculars to my side and step out from my hiding spot.

I'm a thirty-four-year-old woman, not some horny teen.

I shake off the sizzling attraction burning through me and check the gardens before returning inside. The prickle of awareness draws my attention back to his floor. I turn and lift the binoculars.

There he is, perfectly framed by the window. His gaze scorches mine through the binoculars.

Fuck. I quickly run into the building. Embarrassment surges through me, making my face hot and my heart pound. Stupid. So stupid. Now he thinks I'm some kind of crazy lunatic.

Back inside, I put the binoculars in the closet and retreat to Grandma's sewing room. I have masks to make.

An insistent buzzing in my pocket snaps me from my thoughts.

"Hey, Lucy. What's up?" I must sound breathless because Lucy corners me like a shark catching the scent of blood.

"What happened? Don't lie to me. You sound like you just ran a marathon."

"What?" I sputter. "Nothing happened. I'm fine. Just doing some cardio."

"Bullshit." She scoffs into the phone, making me jerk my head away from it. "I know you well enough to know you aren't doing any goddamn cardio during this lockdown. You hate cardio. Period. Spill."

She's caught me. I tell her exactly what happened with the mystery man across the alley. She listens, but I can tell she's building up her reaction for when I stop talking.

"I feel like an idiot." I hide my face in my palm.

Silence. Nothing but silence. That terrifies me.

"Lucy? You still there?"

A burst of laughter echoes through the line. I hold my head away from the phone this time, and her voice comes through clear as a police siren barreling down Broad Street. It's annoying. I wait until her laugher eases and place the phone back against my ear.

"Oh god, girl. You fucked yourself on that one, didn't

you?"

Anxiety rears its ugly head. "What do you mean?"

"Here I was worried he was the perv. Sounds like you won't have to worry about him anymore." She chuckles again but then immediately sobers. "I'm sorry. I don't mean that. This whole lockdown has people going crazy. We're all doing the best we can. Maybe it's better if you stay off the roof for a while."

I sigh. "If only that were an option. I have to take care of my seedlings. Maybe I'll only do a morning and evening watering. The rest of the work can wait."

"Or just do your thing. You do you, girl. Fuck him."

Fuck him. Oh, sweet mercy, the thought alone makes my head swim and my face heat. "Yeah. Fuck him."

"You'd better rein in those hormones. I've been there. But this time is about social distancing and staying safe." She pauses with emphasis. "Besides, he could still be a goddamn serial killer perv."

I facepalm again. "Yes, Mom."

"Smartass. You're lucky my shift starts in an hour. I love ya. Behave."

"Love you too." I disconnect the call and set the phone on the sewing table.

With a sigh, I pull out the printed pattern I found online and start measuring the fabric and cutting pieces. I need something to distract me.

Not that it matters. My subconscious always brings me back to the man with the whiskey eyes.

CHAPTER FIVE
A DRONE AND THE TIGER KING

BEN

LOCKDOWN DAY 12

The files are due in two days. Mr. Kennedy expects them Friday morning. It's Wednesday, April 1. It feels like someone's playing a cruel joke on me. Half the documents I need to finish the report are sitting on the hard drive of my work laptop in my office, twelve blocks away. I need them.

Realistically, I can write up the report and compile what I need from home. But I need to be concise. Everything should be in the report the first time. Pandemic be damned. I still have work to do. I can't let this whole venture fail because of the lockdown. Not when the last ten years I spent building and investing in my multi-million-dollar company are at stake.

I flinch as guilt consumes me. After my conversation with my parents the night before, I turned on the news and regretted it immediately.

New York City is the center of the epidemic in the states. I'm in the middle of a war zone. People are dying. I changed the channel to a kid's cartoon after thirty minutes. The emotionally-charged media only exacerbated the anxiety coursing through me. I pride myself on my ability to think critically, but with everything in such a volatile state, it seems wiser to just walk away. I can't control it.

So I choose to focus on the only thing I can control. My work. Which means I need those papers.

I change into jeans and my running shoes. After I throw

on a light jacket, I grab my keys and step out into the hallway. So far, so good.

It's early afternoon. The streets are vacant. I pass a few people walking, but most of them are carrying groceries or taking their dogs out for a break. I duck my head, afraid the selfish reason for my being out is scrawled across my torso in bold red letters.

After three blocks, I'm confident I can make it to the office and back without any issue. I round the corner and slam into a solid blue wall. A cop.

Damn it.

The cop stumbles back, his hand resting on his holster.

"I'm so sorry." I lift my hands and back up a respectful distance.

"No harm done." He relaxes and drops his hand. "In a hurry, are you?"

"Yeah." I shy away from the conversation because I don't want to lie. I know firsthand that's a quick way to dig yourself a grave.

"Where are you off to in such a hurry?" The cop eyes me from head to toe, his eyes narrowing just a fraction.

"Myrtle Avenue." I edge my way around him.

"That's over by the hospital. You sick?" He rests his hand on the radio hanging from his hip belt.

"No. Just running a quick errand."

The cop shakes his head. "I'm afraid I can't let you go that far. You have to stay in the Heights. Unless it's an emergency. Then you need to call 911 or the hospital directly."

I want to punch something. I was so close. Damn it. "Sir, I understand completely. But this is important."

"Look, people are dying. This isn't the time to be running around the city, acting like everything is normal. The governor and the mayor have declared a state of emergency. You need to go home. And stay home." He pins me with a stare that would do my mother proud. "Now."

I open my mouth to argue. Nearly two weeks cooped up

in my apartment, only allowed to go to the corner market for supplies, and I'm about ready to lose whatever remains of my restraint.

"Where do you live?" he asks, when I don't move.

"Columbia." I don't specify which street, since there's both a Heights and a Place.

He doesn't miss a beat. "Let me see your ID."

"That's not necessary, sir." I stiffen and grind my teeth as I force a smile. "I'll go home right now."

"ID, now." He holds his hand out.

I stifle a groan and pull my wallet from my jacket pocket. After I hand him my ID, he pulls out his pad and writes my information down.

This is absolute bullshit. I should have stayed home, or at least waited until dark. Not sure if that would help my case or hurt it. It's a safe bet being caught after dark trying to sneak through the city during lockdown would land me in jail. I already look like a felon. The last thing the company needs is me getting into trouble with the police department.

When he hands back my ID, I can tell he doesn't trust me. "Phone number?"

I give him my cell number and stuff my hands in my pockets. Irritation pricks at the back of my neck. "Is that all, officer?"

"Yes. Now, go home. We're all in this together."

The hell we are. I nod, unable to trust my own words. I don't want a ticket. I sure as hell don't want him to drag me to the station.

He crosses his arms and waits until I turn and walk back the way I came. I can feel his gaze on me as I walk up the street and turn back toward Columbia Heights. I grumble under my breath during the entire trek back to my apartment. How the hell can I possibly get anything done if I can't access my office?

I wave at the doorman as I enter the building. He returns the greeting. I take the stairs, hoping it will burn off the irritation churning in my gut. The thought of being caged inside the elevator makes my head swim.

By the time I reach my apartment, a nimbus cloud has settled over me. I glare at my laptop on the kitchen table. I should work. But I can't. Whatever motivation I had disappeared the moment that cop stopped me.

Truth is, what's the fucking point? It's not like any of this shit matters now. I can only hope Mr. Kennedy understands the extenuating circumstances. But he's a practical businessman, like me. Whatever hope remained sours in my gut.

I open the cabinet next to the pantry and pull out the bottle of bourbon I keep stashed in the back. I never drink at home or alone. But since I'm already throwing caution to the fucking wind by breaking lockdown restrictions, who cares.

I grab a glass from the cupboard and collapse on the couch. I pour two fingers and toss it back. The sweet burn warms me instantly. I take another. This time the tension in my mind eases as the alcohol drowns it. The blank television screen reflects nearly as well as a mirror. Disgusted by my own reflection, I grab the new remote and turn it on, ignoring the news channels and turning on Netflix.

Good thing I keep my information saved. I can't remember the last time I logged into the streaming service. I scroll aimlessly, wanting something brainless and stupid to block out the inner workaholic raging in the back of my mind.

What the hell? Half of the shows are originals, whatever that means. Some of the older titles I recognize. But, for the most part, I can't differentiate one show from another. I let a few of the previews play, but nothing catches my interest. I purposely skip the documentary suggestions. Ugh, who wants to deal with reality right now?

I pour a third glass of bourbon. The moment it touches my lips, I hear something. I turn off the television. *TAP TAP TAP*. Is someone knocking at the door?

I check. No one at the door.

TAP TAP TAP. I scratch my head. Where's it coming from?

TAP TAP TAP. It sounds like someone knocking on glass. I move closer to the window and draw the sheer curtain back. I blink twice before it registers in my brain.

A white drone hovers outside my window. I glance across the alley. She's sitting on the edge of the rooftop, a controller in her hand. Instead of waving, she taps the glass again with the drone.

When I open the window, she lands the drone perfectly on the ledge. Taped on the top of the drone is a bright blue piece of paper. I glance up.

From this distance, I can just make out the smile on her face. I shake my head and pull the paper from the drone.

I unfold it.

Hello. You look like you could use a friend. 555-5309.

Warmth spreads through me, and I melt at the kind gesture and wave. I wonder about her every time I pass a window, and I search for her, consciously or not. I can't deny my curiosity. But over the past few days, work has distracted me so completely, I forgot about the girl in the garden.

The buzz of the drone interrupts my thoughts. It's hovering again, withdrawing out into the void between us. She navigates the drone back to her rooftop and lands it on the open area by her feet. After picking it up, she waves once more before disappearing into the building.

I look at the paper in my hand. I should've sent my number back to her, but it's too late. I close the window and return to the couch. As I drink my bourbon, I stare at the number scrawled across the paper and wonder if this is a really bad idea.

The humor of the situation strikes me as I add her number to my pathetic contact list. I chuckle at the absurdity of a drone delivering a message. Her ability to problem solve is admirable, and I'm impressed by her commitment to making the first move.

I down the liquor and put the note in the book sitting beside my bed before heading to the bathroom. Maybe a shower will help clear my head. Truth is, I don't know what to say that won't make me sound crazy.

Penelope

Lockdown Day 12

Oh, shit. What did I just do? My heart's racing. I might throw up.

As soon as I'm back in the safety of the house, I collapse against the door, careful not to break the drone in my hand. I set it in the case on the table and wipe my palms on my thighs. Why am I sweating? What's wrong with me?

Uncertainty claws at my chest. What if he's not interested? I pinch my eyes closed and take several deep breaths. My heart is still pounding like a jackhammer. What the hell is wrong with me? Anxiety and nervous energy swirl in the pit of my stomach, and I feel like I'm going to puke.

My phone rings. My heart stops beating. It's him.

I pull the phone out and pray. Then I look at the screen. False alarm. Relief washes over me.

"Hey, Lucy."

"Heya, honey. Just checking on you." She pauses. "Cardio again?" The sarcasm in her voice is more than evident. Damn, she's good.

"Yeah." I know it's pointless to lie to her, but I can't confess what I just did. She'll think I'm a nutjob.

"Bullshit. Been up on that roof again?"

"Maybe."

"Don't lie to me, woman. I have four brothers. I know when someone's lying. I can smell the bullshit a mile off. Spill. What'd he do now?"

I chew my lower lip before I reply, "Nothing."

"Okay. Then what did you do? Did you give him a show? Huh?" She laughs. "This whole time I was worried he's the perv, and it's you I should've been worried about."

"No!" I flop onto the couch. "I just. Well, I did something stupid."

"What'd you do? Can't be that bad if you're telling me you didn't flash him."

"Remember that drone I bought a few weeks ago to take pictures of the roof layout and the cityscape?"

"Did you take naked pictures of him using that drone?" From the tone of her voice, I can't tell whether she's horrified or impressed. "Is he hot? Was it worth it?" Impressed, definitely impressed. Yeah, Lucy's a deviant.

"I did not use it to take naked pictures of him." My attempt at sounding indignant comes off as disappointed. Although, the thought of snapping a picture of him naked has my blood simmering.

"Then what the hell did you do? Spill."

"I sent him a note using the drone."

"What was on the note? A bold confession?"

"My number."

"Your number?" She pauses, and I wonder if she's putting on her shoes to come over and slap me upside the head. "You did that just now?"

"Yeah."

"And he hasn't called you yet?"

"No."

"A text?"

"No."

The silence stretches until it threatens to snap. I can feel the tension building. "He will."

I exhale sharply. I didn't realize I'd been holding my breath. "Do you think so?"

"If he doesn't, he's an idiot. Fuck him."

I smile. It feels good to have Lucy on my team. We haven't been friends for long, but it feels like we've known each other forever. She's got my back. "Fuck him."

Her laughter bubbles through the line. "Girl, you've got it bad. As a nurse, I can't condone any social interaction, given the state of this pandemic, but it sounds like you two need to fuck and get it out of your systems."

"Are you always so crass?"

"That's a stupid question. I'm going to pretend you didn't ask me such a ridiculous question."

"Thanks, Lucy."

"Of course, hon. I gotta run. Text me as soon as he makes a move."

I roll my eyes. "Now who's a perv?"

"And you love me for it. Later."

"Bye." I draw out the word and end the call.

The stillness of the house is too much. I flip on the television and log into my Netflix account, hoping they uploaded the new season of something I like. I need a distraction.

After five minutes of aimless searching, I settle on a movie I've seen a million times. A nineties rom-com set in Chicago, starring Sandra Bullock. I lose myself in the story, and the city around me fades away.

PING. I grab the phone and unlock it on reflex. I tear my eyes from the TV long enough to read the text.

Hi, neighbor. Unknown number. Blue bubble. An iMessage. I sit up straight. It must be him.

Penelope. This is so awkward. My thundering heart disagrees completely. This is the most thrilling adventure I've had in weeks, months even.

?

My name is Penelope.

Ah. I'm Ben. Nice to put a name to the gardener.

I blink at the screen. *Ben.* And he's quippy. I smile at the screen and warmth floods my body.

Spending lockdown alone? I regret the question the moment I send it.

Yeah. You?

Yeah.

How's the garden coming?

He's been watching. The thought makes me smile. *Slow, but I have sproutlings already.*

That's great. What are you growing?

Tomatoes, peas, peppers, lettuce, and onions.

Impressive. What else do you like to do besides gardening?

Sewing, painting, taking walks in the park, window shopping, going to the theater. You?

Running.

That's all you do for fun?

I work a lot.

Lockdown must be rough.

It is.

I chew on my lip, my brow furrows. *What do you do for work?*

I own a business.

What kind.

We manufacture and sell supplies to large corporations.

Sounds evasive.

I don't want to bore you with my work.

What are you doing right now? I didn't mean for it to sound provocative, but I worry it might come across as such.

Watching Netflix.

Me too. What show/movie?

Nothing yet. I never watch TV. What do you recommend?

I stare at the television. The rom-com on the screen is comforting for me, but I doubt it's something he would want to watch. I click on the remote, taking me back to the main screen. I see Tiger King under recommended viewing.

My friend told me to watch Tiger King.

What's it about?

I don't know, she said it's a train wreck.

It looks like a documentary.

I grin when the idea hits me. *Why don't we watch it together?*

Lockdown, remember?

*Yes, I know. I mean you watch it there. I'll watch it here. We can text each other as we watch it. *Smiley emoji**

.

..

...

I watch the dots appear and disappear. My heart is in my throat. I want to keep talking to him.

Let's do it.

I punch my fist in the air. *I'm gonna grab a drink. I'll text you when I'm ready to start.*

Okay.

I run to the kitchen and grab a beer. If this show is anything like what Lucy said it was, I'm going to need to break out the hard liquor. I plop onto the couch and pull a blanket across my lap.

Ready. I text him, and then I press play.

After one episode, we're both riveted and appalled. It's going to be a long night, but at least I have someone to share it with.

CHAPTER SIX
MAINTAINING SANITY

BEN

LOCKDOWN DAY 13

The warm, strong coffee clears my head. I lean against the window frame and stare out over the neighboring rooftops.

She must still be asleep. We watched the entire disastrous documentary in one sitting, which put us well past midnight. I can't be sure whether the show was a clever distraction or a horrendous commentary on humanity. For a short period of time, I forgot my problems. If that was the intent, they succeeded. When I fell asleep, I dreamt of big cats and the sweet kitten in the building next door.

Oh, god. Something's wrong with me. I shake my head and sip my coffee before turning back to my laptop and the tabletop littered with papers. I have twenty-four hours to finish sorting and organizing this chaos. Mr. Kennedy expects the best, and I intend to give him just that.

I reach for my phone and open the text box. Shit. Don't text her. I lock the phone again and flip it over, ignoring the urge to read through our messages from last night. It's all innocent conversation, mostly inane observations on the show and the vivid cast of characters. She sent twice as many messages as I did and didn't seem to mind. Neither did I. But now I crave more.

After a few minutes, I fall into a rhythm sorting documents and verifying information in the database. The morning disintegrates under this newfound productivity.

My stomach grumbles, and I finally glance at the clock. It's already two! I stand and stretch, sneaking a glimpse out the window. Still no sign of her. I shove away the disappointment.

I make a sandwich and grab some chips. I'm nearly finished when my phone rings. I snatch it up and see Mom's face. When I answer the video chat, I force a smile.

"Hey, Mom."

"Benjamin. How are you? Are you okay?" She tilts the phone, so I see mostly the ceiling and the top half of her head. I refrain from rolling my eyes. She still hasn't quite gotten the hang of technology.

"I'm fine." I sigh. "Mom, tilt the phone down. I can't see your face."

She tilts it a bit more, and now, I have a full Blair Witch viewpoint of my mother's face. "Is this better?"

I shake my head. "Yeah, Mom. How are you and Dad?"

"Oh, we're doing fine. They've closed the community center." Mom clicks her tongue. "Dad's disappointed there won't be any bingo for a few weeks."

"You can always have him organize the shop if he needs something to keep him busy."

"That's what I told him." She sighs. "The governor is closing down all non-essential businesses and events." I can hear the exhaustion in her voice. Since they retired, my parents need activities to get them out of the house. I'm not sure what will happen if they're locked up for an extended period of time. Forty-five years of marriage takes a toll. I don't know how they do it.

"Yeah. It's been pretty quiet here since they shut New York down." I push past the subject of the virus and the lockdown into a more familiar conversation. "Have you spoken to Rick?"

"I called him last night. They're doing well. The schools in their state are closed too. The boys are driving him crazy." She laughs.

My nephews are both under ten. Their new school

schedule has disrupted the entire family's routine. Rick's last email said they do most of their classwork online, but it's hell to keep them focused during the day. "I'm sure that's a challenge for everyone right now."

"Both Rick and Kate are working from home during the shutdown. I don't know how they balance working and helping the boys with school."

"It'll take a week or two to figure it out." I glance at the mess on the table. We're all trying to figure this shit out. "How's Susan?"

"She hasn't called me in a few days. Last I heard, she was working on a curriculum to use online for her students." Mom's expression beams pride. "I hope she has everything she needs. I hate that she lives on the other side of the state."

"I'm sure Susan has friends who can help her out if she needs it."

"I worry about you two the most, you know. Being so far away from home. Not having anyone to take care of you." Her lip trembles. "Especially you. You've always been such a loner."

Shit. "I know, Mom. I'm doing fine, I promise. I've got this under control. How's that new quilt coming along?"

She brightens at the change in topic and launches into a description of the two quilts she's making for her grandsons. Good, she needs a distraction. We all do.

After five minutes, she lets me go, promising to have Dad call me once he comes in from the garage. He's out there tinkering with something in a valiant effort to give Mom some space. I plug the phone in and take my plate to the kitchen.

I dive back into work and send off a few emails. I need whatever documents I can get my hands on. Andrew keeps backups of some of them on the external server. I'll have him sort them and send me what I need.

My phone rings. I jog over to the couch and grab it from the coffee table. Video call request. Garden girl. *Penelope.* I should change the name. Contradictory waves of uncertainty and need zing through me and land like rocks in the pit of my stomach. My thumb hovers over the green button when the call ends.

A text pings through a moment later.

Sorry. I hit the wrong button.

I can't tell if I'm more disappointed or relieved. *No problem. How are you?*

I return to the table and sit down. I need to work, otherwise, I'll just sit and slowly descend into madness, watching those three dots flash on the screen. After a few moments, the phone pings again.

I'm good. Thanks for hanging out last night.

I enjoyed it.

Me too. Another message comes through. *Want to do it again?*

I have some work to finish. I hit send accidentally. Shit.

As I continue typing out my response, she replies. *Oh, yeah, of course. Sorry to interrupt.*

What about Saturday night. Seven. You pick the movie.

It's a date. The dots appear and disappear several times.

I stare at the words, and my lips twist in a half-smile.

Sorry, I didn't mean date *date, just well, you know I put it on the calendar.* She inserts a little facepalm emoji at the end.

It's a date *date then.* respond before I can second-guess myself. Truth is, I want it to be a real date. I want to know more about her. I want more than that, and the thought should terrify me. Instead, anticipation and excitement bubble inside me like lava beneath a dormant volcano.

I watch the dots play across the screen for a few minutes, but nothing comes through. What has come over me? I don't even know this girl.

But I want to, and I'm not sure what to do with that knowledge, except bury it beneath a mountain of work to deal with later.

Penelope

LOCKDOWN DAY 13

My hands ache from cutting fabric and sewing all morning. Now they're shaking. Damn it. I stare at the phone on the kitchen counter. A jumble of electricity zings through me. Saturday. Movie. Date.

I squeal and do a little dance around the kitchen. I admit I was a bit worried. Last night was the most fun I'd had in a while, and that's saying something. Two weeks without any physical or social interaction. I've had phone calls with family and friends, but this is different. This is new and shiny. I'm terrified it'll fall apart with the slightest encouragement.

He's definitely not an optimist if his commentary on the documentary is any indicator. He's a realist with a jaded eye. Everyone's guilty. Everyone's hiding something. I chuckle. He's direct and bold, even as a man of few words. His limited responses drove my curiosity insane. I wanted conversation and conjecture. That's nearly impossible through text messaging. I almost called him. But I chickened out.

What does he sound like? Does he have an accent? Is he as reserved on the phone as he is through messages? I pace the floor. I shouldn't have hung up the video chat. It was an honest mistake. But now I wonder if it wasn't my subconscious pushing me.

I grab the phone. I want to call him, but he's working. Give the man some space. I groan. What the hell is wrong with me?

Maybe I should go up and check on the garden. Yeah.

My phone rings, and I scream and nearly drop it. I catch the name on the screen and try to control my now racing heart.

"Hey, Lucy."

"Hey, hon. How are you holdin' up?"

"Fine." I bubble with excitement but hesitate. Lucy doesn't trust anyone. I fear if I tell her, I'll get a lecture on all the pervs in New York. "I've been working on those masks you asked for. Nearly got a big box full."

"Damn, girl. You're on a roll."

I laugh. "Not like I have much else to do other than sew and work on the garden."

"You can always start putting your touches on the brownstone. I mean, it is your place now."

Sadness seeps in. I miss Grandma and Grandpa terribly. While I boxed up most of their stuff and donated the rest, the house still holds remnants of their presence. I'm afraid to change anything. If I do, it's like I'm erasing them from existence. "I dunno."

"Listen. I know what you're thinking. I had the same problem when my grandma passed. I couldn't get rid of anything. It all reminded me of her. But, trust me, their memory isn't tied to stuff. It's in your heart. Live your life, Penelope. Your grandparents wanted you to have their place. Make it yours."

I nod. "Yeah, I know. I just miss 'em. Being cooped up isn't helping. I miss walking in the park. I miss having you over for Chinese food and movies."

She scoffs. "You and me both, sister. I'm damn near pulling my hair out here at the hospital. We're bringing in staff from all over, trying to fill the gaps. I'd give anything for a night off."

"I'm sorry. I shouldn't be bitching about this when you're stuck working on the front lines. You're my hero, you know that."

"It sucks all around. I know. Hopefully we'll get all this shit calmed down before long. I need a girls' night after this. Hell, I may need a girls' vacation to a deserted island with a cabana boy and endless mojitos."

"Done. It'll be my treat to reward the city's finest nurse."

She laughs. "Yeah. Doesn't feel that way, but I'm glad at least one person appreciates me."

"You're damn right I appreciate you. You're the only one who calls me every day to make sure I'm not going insane."

"Someone's gotta keep an eye on you." Lucy pauses. "Speaking of keeping an eye on you, whatever happened to the perv on the seventh floor? Did he call?"

Heat floods my face. "Well, he…uh." Shit. I was supposed to call her if he messaged me. In all the excitement, I forgot to tell my best friend. Damn.

"He called you?" Her voice rises an octave.

"No, he didn't call. He texted."

"And?" She draws the word out. "What the fuck happened? Spill it. Tell me everything."

"We texted for a bit while we watched a documentary together. Well, in our respective residences, but we texted while we watched the show." I told her about the documentary, and his commentary on it.

Silence. "Shit." She sounds surprised. "Does this man have a name?"

"Ben."

"Ben?" The name rolls around on her tongue for a moment. "That's it. No last name."

"No. Why?"

"No reason." Lucy always has a reason for things.

"You were going to have your brother look him up, weren't you?"

Lucy sputters. "I don't know what you're talking about. I would never have Joey abuse his powers like that."

"You've had him vet every man you've seen in the past two years. You told me yourself."

"Alright, fine. You caught me. It's better to be safe than sorry, Penelope. You have Joey's number down at the 99th precinct. If Ben turns out to be a creep, call him. I'm serious."

I shake my head. "What do I have to do to prove to you that he's not a perv or a creep?"

Lucy doesn't miss a beat. "Full background check, run his prints, and vetted references."

"You need to relax. He's not a serial killer."

"That you know of." Lucy sighs. "Just be careful, huh?"

"Always." I love this woman. She's the only reason I decided to give life in the city a chance. I'm so glad I did. "We have a date on Saturday night."

"A date? What the hell do you mean a date?" Her indignance makes her voice crack.

"We're gonna watch a movie while we do a video chat."

"Uh-huh." She's holding back, I can tell by her tone.

"What?"

"Nothing." I hate it when she does this. It's a sure sign she's about to lay down the mom law. "If he suggests porn, run like hell. I'm serious. Nothing good can come from that. Trust me."

It's on the tip of my tongue to ask her how she could have firsthand knowledge of this when she swears. "What?"

"I gotta run. Looks like I'm starting my shift early today." She sighs again. "I love ya. Stay out of trouble, please."

"Trouble? Me?" I simper in my best sweet and innocent Southern belle impersonation. "Stay safe out there. Love you, too."

After the call ends, I grab a glass of water and head for the rooftop. I need some air and sunlight. Reality is hitting too close to home, and right now, I just need the open sky overhead, a taste of freedom, and maybe a glimpse of Ben.

CHAPTER SEVEN
MOVIE NIGHT

BEN

LOCKDOWN DAY 15

Where are they? I shift through the box of files and frown. They have to be here. Where the hell else would they be? I slump back and rake my hand through my hair, tempted to tear out the overgrown mess.

After my momentary pity party, I dove back into work. I finished the proposal for Mr. Kennedy and had it delivered to his apartment by 10:00 a.m. Friday morning, as promised. His phone call at six o'clock that same evening demolished whatever confidence I had.

The yearly finance reports were included, of course, but he requested the quarterly financial reports as well, since they break down the spending to income ratio by department. Why wouldn't he? Any sane businessman would do the same before agreeing to merge two multi-million-dollar companies. I want to beat my head against the table.

I turn the box to read the label I've read a dozen times in the last few hours. *It won't change if it hasn't already, you idiot.* The dark bold script says Financial Records on the side of the box. I brought it home with me to do some last-minute research for the final merger. But that was back before the whole lockdown started. I'm glad I did, but now, I'm kicking myself for not verifying it had everything I needed. I know all the files are on the office server, but I can't access it from home without my work laptop. It's like a culmination of a series of stupid little missteps led to this moment. I want to take my lighter to the whole fucking mess and watch it burn.

With a few classy swear words, I shoot to my feet and pace the length of the apartment. I wish I could go for a run. I need to burn off the energy coursing through me. It's been simmering beneath the surface for two weeks. Even my trips to the market and taking the garbage down to the dumpster aren't enough to take the edge off anymore. Is this what a caged animal feels like? Images of tigers pacing their cages flash in my mind. Tigers and zoos in Oklahoma and insane murder plots.

Fucking Tiger King. I remember watching it, but that's not what sticks with me. No. It's her. We shared that horrific experience, just like we're sharing this whole lockdown with the city. Hell, with the world.

It's a goddamn nightmare. I continue to avoid the news and social media. I don't need that shit piled on top of my already spiraling sanity. My only updates come from my parents, who call me more and more frequently now. I appreciate their concern, but I'd rather not have to rehash the same shit every day. I have no fucking clue how this will end. All I know is that I need to get my work laptop if I'm going to get anything else done. Amid all this chaos, work is the only thing keeping me grounded. Take that away and I'm fucked.

That's not completely true. I glance out the window at the neighboring rooftop shrouded in darkness. Maybe something good can come from this shitshow.

My phone pings. I grab it from the table. I smile as I read her simple, bright greeting.

Hello!

Hey there, sunshine. I have no idea why I called her that. I groan at my inability to communicate with her.

I'm ready for our date.

I blink at the message in confusion for a second before I glance at the time. Holy shit, it's nearly seven-thirty! *Sorry. Yeah. I'm ready.*

My phone vibrates. Incoming video call. I swallow the lump in my throat and answer it. Her smile lights up the screen.

"Hi! Figured this would make it easier to watch a movie together. It's hard to text and watch at the same time." She beams at me, and all I can do is stare.

Fuck, she's prettier than I remember. "Whatever works," I reply before realizing I never said hello. "How are you?"

"Me?" She seems surprised I asked. "I'm doing good. Been sewing masks all week. Phew. It's exhausting. I think I'll have to ice my hand down from cutting out all that fabric." She chuckles.

My heart flips over twice. She's the warm, soft, sweet center of the cinnamon roll. I bet she tastes just as delicious too. My mouth waters at the thought. I groan and force the temptation from my mind. Sweet sunshine doesn't mix well with brooding workaholic.

"What are the masks for?" I ask, unwilling to board the train of thought currently barrelling through my body at ninety miles an hour.

She launches into a huge explanation I vaguely hear. I'm too distracted memorizing her features. The soft curl of her dark hair over her left shoulder. The way she flips it when she's talking almost absentmindedly. Are her eyes more green or blue? I can't tell in the lighting from the video quality. Her shimmering lips mesmerize me. Is that lip gloss? She doesn't look like she's wearing makeup. The natural look suits her perfectly. The smattering of freckles only enhances the already vivid girl-next-door look she has going on. I wonder if her skin is as smooth as it looks.

"I promised to have the masks done by next week and deliver them." She takes a deep breath. "Lucy says they're desperate for whatever they can get their hands on. But she thinks we'll need them ourselves soon, thanks to the mayor's new decree."

I shake my head from the clouded thoughts and focus on her words. "New decree?"

"Yeah, didn't you see the news today?" She cocked her head.

"I avoid it."

She smiles again, and it's like a kick to the chest. "Smart. It's a lot of scaremongering and bullshit anyway. No one seems to have any idea what's going on." She sighs. "Anyway, yeah, the mayor said they're considering making masks a requirement to even leave your home now. I guess we'll find out next week."

"Yeah." I shake my head. Reality rears its ugly head, and I want to scream. Instead, I focus on her voice. Silky and sweet, without a trace of that distinct, harsh New York lilt, lingering on her vowels. Where is she from? Most people in the city are from somewhere else. She's luring me in, and so help me, I'm not resisting.

"If you need a mask or two, I can make them for you."

"Thanks. That'd be great."

Her expression glows. "Any request for fabric?"

"Not really."

"I'll make it a surprise then." She grins.

Normally surprises set my teeth on edge. I hate them with a fierce passion surpassed only by my hatred for traitors and broccoli.

"Not a fan of surprises, are you?"

I force a smile. "How could you tell?"

"The look of utter horror on your face gave it away." She laughs. "Don't worry. I won't make you a mask with dicks on it or anything."

My jaw drops. "With what on it?"

"Dicks. Tiny penises. Almost like a paisley pattern if you're far enough away, but up close, yup, it's definitely a mask with dicks on it." Her laugher is infectious.

I chuckle. "I didn't even know that was a thing. Who would want a fabric with that all over it?"

"You'd be shocked at the different types of fabric available." She sighs and shakes her head.

"I'm sure." I walk to the fridge and pull out a beer.

"It's almost eight o'clock. Still want to watch a movie?" She takes a sip of something from a tall glass.

"Yeah, sure." I point at the glass. "What's that you're drinking?"

"Hard cider." She takes another sip, and her sound of delight ricochets through me. If I didn't know better, I'd say it was a moan. "My favorite. The shop I get them from delivers now, so I'm stocked up. What are you drinking?"

I pop the top of my Yuengling and hold the bottle up to the camera.

"Mmmm, good shit right there. My grandpa drank one every day. Called it his medicine."

"Sounds like a smart man."

"He was." The sparkle in her eyes dims. "I miss him."

Fuck. He died. Goddamn it. "I'm sorry for your loss."

"Yeah, he and Grandma passed in November last year."

"You were close to them?" I stumble through the words, unsure of how the hell we got on this subject in the first place. Grief is not one of my strong suits. I don't know what the hell to do with most emotions, but that one is a fucking enigma. I'd take on a boardroom full of rich vultures before offering comfort to a grieving woman.

"Yeah." She glances off into the distance. "They lived here for years, and I visited often."

Silence falls between us, heavy and awkward. She takes another sip of her cider and turns back to face the camera.

"Okay, enough sad talk. Movie time." She bounces back quickly.

I'm stunned at the shift but glad she changed the direction of the conversation. I'm shit at talking about emotions, never mind knowing what the hell to do with them. I clear my throat.

"Yeah, which one did you want to watch?"

"*The Mummy.*" Her eyes glow with delight.

"Wait, that new flick with Cruise in it?" I scowl. She doesn't seem like the type for something that…weird.

Her face scrunches up in a look of disgust. "Hell no! I'm talking about the one with Brendan Fraser." She sighs and bats her lashes at the mention of the actor's name. "It's one of my favorites."

"I couldn't tell." I deadpan. The girl practically swoons at the thought of a fictional character. I shake my head. "Is it on Netflix?"

"Yeah, queue it up!" The phone bounces as she collapses onto the couch. She sets the phone on the coffee table, so we can still talk while we watch the movie.

Ten minutes into the movie and I'm riveted. Not by the movie. By her. She's completely enchanting.

I can see her mouth the words as the characters deliver their lines. She pulls a pillow into her lap and wraps her arms around it when Rick appears on the screen in all his cleanshaven glory. When he nearly kisses the heroine, Evelyn, by the fire, I note Penelope's reaction. She leans forward, her mouth parted, eyes glassy. I want to laugh, but I can't. As the film progresses, I'm drawn into the story while still marking her reactions carefully.

Rick's character is everything I'm not. Confident and charismatic. Hero material, even if he is a bit reckless and charming to a fault. He resembles my business partner, Evan, more than me, but I don't want to examine that comparison too closely.

I can see why Penelope is drawn to the film. It has a great mix of thrilling action and daring adventure. The dash of romance complements the story as a whole. The acting isn't too over the top, and there are some great one-liners. Even the heroine has caught my attention, but only because she reflects so much of what I see in Penelope, even in the short time I've known her.

What the hell am I saying? This is the first time we've spoken. We haven't even shared the same air! Wait, we did once. But it wasn't enough. No, I need more than this limited interaction.

Once the credits roll, I lean back on the couch, silent, waiting for Penelope to speak. The final kiss lingers in my mind as the music swells in the background. I can't remember a single, solitary moment in my life when I craved a kiss, one simple physical interaction, so desperately.

"So, what do you think?" She grins through the video. "Pretty good, huh?"

I fold my arms across my chest, ignoring the pull of desire twisting in my gut. "A decent adventure flick."

She narrows her gaze. "It's got everything. Action. Adventure. Romance. Mummies!"

I show my hands in supplication. "You win. It's a great movie."

"Better." She picks up the phone, bringing her flushed cheeks closer to the camera. She flips her hair to the side and twists it. "Thanks for hanging out with me tonight. I enjoyed it."

"Me too." There's tension pulsing between us. I can feel it, even though we're in separate buildings. I want to say something, but my mind short circuits with every breath.

"Can we do it again next week?" She's breathless and hopeful and so fucking adorable.

I shouldn't. I can't stand this distance between us. I want her company. I want her here with me. Fucking pandemic. Fucking lockdown. I run my fingers through my hair.

"Yeah, sure." The words slip from my mouth without permission. Damn it.

"Yay!" She bounces up and down on the other end of the video in what I can only assume is a joyful expression of excitement. "I'll text you tomorrow, okay?"

"Yup." It's safer to keep my responses short. I can't trust myself right now. I'll say something incredibly stupid.

She winks and waves. "Goodnight, Ben. Sleep well."

"Goodnight, Penelope." I disconnect the call.

With a groan, I toss the phone aside and retreat into the bedroom. I need a cold shower. How can one woman cause me such discomfort when I haven't even touched her?

PENELOPE

LOCKDOWN DAY 15

My heart is doing laps in an Olympic-sized pool of champagne bubbles. I chew on my lip and stare at the phone in my hands. I could lie and say it's because of the movie. It is my favorite. But, deep inside, I know it's because of him. I feel lighter than I have in ages. Effervescent and carbonated like I could just float off into the sky on a giant soap bubble.

But bubbles pop. That's a fact. It's also my biggest fear.

This whole situation is surreal. Grandma and Grandpa dying. Inheriting their estate and this amazing historic building. I hug the pillow closer to my chest. The lockdown. Meeting Ben. BEN.

Oh, man. Ben. I think his voice branded me. I'm almost positive it will leave a permanent scar. I squeeze the pillow tighter. I wasn't lying when I told him I enjoyed spending time with him. Even if we were separated by a physical distance.

This new, shiny friendship stands in deep contrast to the darkness of the uncertainty and chaos surrounding the world. I pick up the phone again and hesitate. I didn't want to hang up. It would have been nice to just have him there. No conversation needed. Just a soul on the other end of the line who needs the connection as much as I do.

I shrug off the blanket and get up from the couch. The soft patter of rain on the window echoes in the living room. I put on my raincoat and head up to the roof. There's supposed to be storms all night and into the next few days. I need to make sure the garden is secure. The last thing I need is my plants drowning in the downpour.

On the roof, the rain pelts my face. I race to ensure the covers are secure on the raised beds and tuck a few items into the shed before I lock it. I glance at Ben's windows. The lights are still on.

Why are you being a creep? I shake my head. Get inside before you catch a cold. I almost laugh at the stupidity of the thought. How ironic would that be, catching a cold while in quarantine to protect yourself from catching another virus? Is this reality? Not that you can catch a virus from the rain. Oh, my god, I'm rambling in my own head. Shut. Up.

His shadow passes by the window. I can see his outline perfectly through the backlit, sheer curtain. He's so broad; he nearly fills the frame. He disappears for a moment, only to reappear in the window by the fire escape. The curtain flutters for a moment before I can see him completely. Oh. My. God. That curtain is sheer too.

He lifts the towel in his hand and dries his hair. At this angle, I can only see the curve of his hip and his ass. Oh, sweet mercy. That ass. My hands flex as though I can imagine the warm globes under my palms. I shake my head to get the rain from my eyes. If I blink, he could disappear. What a tragedy that would be.

He tosses the towel onto the bed. My mouth waters as my gaze rakes over his broad shoulders and defined curves. My cheeks heat, and I hold my breath. I can almost hear his voice in my mind. That husky rumble that leaves me questioning my sanity.

I lean closer, wanting to scramble to the edge of the roof for a better view. But I'm horrified at myself. Am I this desperate? Ugh, I know I should turn away. I should go back inside and forget about this. But I can't.

Ben disappears from view and disappointment soaks through me like the rain. Damn it.

I run back into the building and hang my wet jacket in the entryway near the radiator to drip dry on the rubber mat. My pants are soaked. I hang them over the laundry basket and head for the shower. I'm not sure if I need a hot one to shake the chill of the April rain shower or a cold one to stop the hormones raging through my body.

I settle for a tepid lukewarm temperature. I'm all about compromise, but it seems my body has a will of its own when it comes to Ben. My skin tingles, oversensitive and hot. The picture of his bare backside lingers in my mind like a flash of lightning branded into my retinas. I feel dirty. I feel naughty. But even more than that, I feel alive.

For the first time in weeks, even months, there's something other than uncertainty. There's hope. There's need. There's chemistry. It's there. I can feel it sparking between us. My heart races at the possibilities, the tension pulling me in.

Just like every time Rick looks at Evie in the movie we watched. There's a magnetism that pulls them together. I can't chase these thoughts. If I do, I'll drive myself mad.

I finish my shower and dry off quickly. After I pull on my fleece pajamas and curl up in bed, I turn on a movie for background noise. The hum of a period drama I've watched a hundred times soothes me.

I clutch my phone in my hand. Should I text him? He's probably asleep. I tap my finger on the phone case. Maybe I should tell him about his curtains.

I nod and unlock my phone.

Hey.

After a few moments, he responds. *Hey.*

I don't want to sound like a creep or anything, but you should get better curtains.

.

..

...

Those three dots would be the absolute death of me, I swear.

How did you come to this realization?

His reply leaves me stunned. Is he drawing me out?

I went to check on my plants. And I saw you.

You saw me.

Yes. In the window. Naked.

.

..

...

And?

I stare at his response. What does that mean? And? And what? I sputter for a moment, trying to figure out what he means. Finally, I respond in the only way I can.

Get some good curtains. Or just stop standing naked in front of a window!

Did you enjoy the view?

Wait. I blink. Is he…flirting with me right now? I mean, we had a lovely evening chatting and watching a movie together, but there wasn't any flirting. Even though I wouldn't have minded it. I mean, technically, it was the first time we actually spoke, but that's not weird. People flirt with strangers all the time. Right? I mean, it happens in movies and books, why can't it happen in real life?

Then why can't I respond? My mind goes completely blank. The phone shakes in my hand. No, that's me shaking. Oh, god. What do I say? I don't want to mess this up.

I plead the Fifth. I hit send.

So, you're afraid you're going to incriminate yourself if you answer truthfully?

I was trying to be a good neighbor.

By spying on me.

I was taking care of my plants. You're the one standing naked by a window with sheer curtains at night in a fucking city.

So defensive.

Bite me.

Was that an offer?

I think my heart just gave out. I feel it pulsing in my chest, but it's like all the blood diverted to my nether regions and forgot to send a memo to my brain.

For what? I reply.

Use your imagination.

Indulge me.

Were you wearing lip gloss tonight?

What does that have to do with anything?

Just answer the question.

I shake my head. Lip gloss. What the hell? How was this even flirting? Is he broken?

Watermelon. Why?

Suits you. Thanks for the heads up about the window. I'll take care of that tomorrow.

You're welcome.

Okay, I'm really confused now. What's going on?

Goodnight.

Night.

I set the phone aside. What just happened? I was convinced the conversation made a sexy turn, but then he slams the breaks on with a weird question about my lip gloss. I'm so confused. Agitated with myself and the strange shift of events, I focus on the television instead.

The more I learn about Ben, the more questions I have. What a strange, sexy man. Maybe we've both been locked up for too long.

CHAPTER EIGHT
MISANTHROPE

BEN

LOCKDOWN DAY 16

I hit ignore on the phone. Four missed calls so far today. This time, it's my parents. I can't bring myself to care. I should talk to them. It's not like they did anything wrong, but honestly, I'm at a breaking point. If I can't get the files I need, the whole merger falls apart.

The sunlight glints off of the rooftop through the sheer curtains. I ignore the pull to go to the window and search for her. Yeah, that's right. I'm ignoring her as well as my parents.

After last night, I can't do it. I thought I could. I hoped she would be an idle distraction, someone to banter with as we wait for the world to reopen. My chest tightens with guilt. I want more than I should. But that entails giving more than I can at the moment. A girl like her deserves more than what I can offer her. I'm already committed to my job.

This lockdown is nothing but a speedbump in the span of my career and the future of my business. I can't afford to derail it for something as distracting and intoxicating as a fling. Her wide eyes full of hope and optimism haunted me all night. And the lack of sleep is wearing on my already exposed nerves.

I didn't ask for this. As much as I try to deny it, I enjoy her company and the conversation. I crave it. My fingers itch to send her a message and pick up where we ended last night.

With a sharp exhale, I rake my hand through my hair and pace the length of the apartment. My gaze flickers to the cigarettes sitting on the table by the door. No, one a day. I can do this.

What the hell was she doing on the roof last night in that storm anyway? The thought of her watching me has my cock aching. Did she like what she saw? Why would she tell me she saw me?

There are blinds in my room, but I never use them. What's the point? Privacy, obviously. I shake my head. Part of me is glad I don't use them. She saw me, and that knowledge makes me hard.

A thousand wicked thoughts flood my mind. But even in the short span of time I've known her, I know her motives for telling me were purely innocent. I scoff. She probably hid her face and retreated inside the moment she realized I was naked.

What if I had known she was watching? My eyes close, and I picture it in my mind. I can't imagine I would have acted on my impulse to tease her. But if I had let it play out, would it have sent her running? Even her texts began innocently enough, as though she would never fantasize about a man she barely knows. Oh, but she walked right into it.

Bite me. Oh, my god. I nearly lost all reason at those words. I'm not kinky. Not even remotely. But the press of teeth against skin, oh fuck. I shiver at the thought.

Her innocent snarky comment brought a buried desire raging to the surface. The thought of leaving a trail of bruising kisses along the column of her pale throat pushed me into delirium. The taste and smell of her infiltrate my imagination. *Watermelon.*

Yes. Sweet and refreshing. A delicious treat on a sweltering summer's day. I could almost taste it.

Which is exactly why I ended the conversation. I couldn't bear the torment. Even though we live in neighboring buildings, with the lockdown we might as well be in two different universes.

The irony of the whole situation would have been comical if it hadn't hit so close to the bullseye.

I spent the night replaying our conversation before the movie. Her voice, soothing and silken, wrapped around me like a blanket. But I tossed and turned half the night, unable to sate the need coursing through me. Desperate, I'd taken myself in hand. The relief was short-lived and left me feeling like a pervert.

Fuck it. I grab the pack of cigarettes and the lighter before heading to the fire escape. Outside, the breeze encircles me, and I close my eyes, savoring the touch of spring in the air. Normally, I would have just gone for a run to burn this mixture of stress and need from my system. Maybe I should just order a damn treadmill and be done with it.

I light the cigarette. The nicotine hits my system in a wave of instantaneous relief, and I slump against the brick outside the window.

It's nearly one in the afternoon, and her rooftop is empty. The rain stopped an hour ago, allowing the sun to peek through the clouds as they dissipate. I frown and shake my head. How fucking desperate am I? Even for a little glimpse of her. I take a drag and let the smoke burn her from my mind.

Ping. I reach for the phone automatically. It's her again. I unlock the phone and scan the last three messages I purposely avoided reading earlier.

Hey.

Just checking on you.

Can we talk about last night?

I hang my head and close my eyes. I don't want to talk about it. The thought of addressing whatever is simmering between us might breathe life into it. It'd be better if we let it rest, or better yet, die.

Hi. I'm fine but busy. Working today. Talk later.

I hit send and ignore the pang in my chest at avoiding her. I should tell her the truth. I suck at relationships, friendship, or otherwise.

*Okay. I'm here if you change your mind. *Smiley Emoji**

Thanks.

I slip the phone in my pocket and finish my cigarette. Back inside, I shut the window and wash up. With some water splashed on my face, I stare at my reflection in the mirror.

"You're an idiot." I shake my head. "Yeah, tell me something I didn't already know."

In the kitchen, I snatch a beer from the fridge and sit at the table to boot up the laptop. I'll send an email to the group and see if they can offer solutions to this mess with the yearly financials. If not, well, I'll cross that bridge tomorrow. Today, I'll try to find a way around it.

My attention drifts out the window to her rooftop. I pull the curtain across the window and grunt. She's nothing but a pretty distraction, and work comes first.

PENELOPE

LOCKDOWN DAY 17

"**H**ey, how are you holding up?" I beam at Lucy through the video on my phone.

She shakes her head, and her lopsided ponytail bobs precariously. "Ugh, I don't know how many more of these long nights I can take. I'm getting too old for this shit."

"You're not that old." I laugh. "Seriously, you make it sound like you should be put in a nursing home."

"Tell that to my back." She arches dramatically and groans. "I don't want to talk about work. That shit's depressing." She zeroes in on my face, and all I can see on the screen are her bright blue eyes. "What I wanna know is what happened during your date the other night? I mean, how does that even work?"

"What?" I shrug, and my face warms. "It was nice. We chatted a bit and then left the video call on while we watched a movie?"

"Porn? Was it porn?" Lucy's grinning like the Joker.

"Oh my god, really? Porn? Why the hell would I watch porn with a complete stranger? I don't even watch porn!"

"I've seen your Tumblr page. That's borderline porn."

I wave her off. "Whatever. Yours is ten times worse. Also, you need to lay off the ReyLo fan fics, they're affecting your taste in men."

"Don't judge me." She sniffs. "Besides, I'm not the one who's in a complicated relationship with her building neighbor, who could very well be the son of the Son of Sam."

I sigh. "He's not a serial killer. He's really sweet."

"Oh, I'm sure he is." Lucy eyes me warily. "So, what movie did you make that poor sap watch?"

"*The Mummy.*"

Lucy rolls her eyes. "You might want to just wear a sign. Hi, I'm Penelope. I'm thirty-four. I'm a hopeless romantic who has an affinity for alpha males."

"Don't be so dramatic." I shift in my seat. "He enjoyed it as much as I did. I think."

"You think?" Lucy leans closer to the screen. "What's that supposed to mean?"

"It means everything was fine until I fucked up." I glance away, trying to ignore the sting of the memory.

"What happened?" Lucy's tone is firm, but I can tell she's worried about me.

I launch into my story, explaining how I went to the roof and saw him naked through the window. But when I told her about my message to him, recommending he use his curtains, Lucy's responding laughter consumes the next five minutes of our conversation. When she finally wipes her eyes and sighs, I can't help but smile.

"Are you done laughing?"

"Oh, honey, what have you done to that poor boy?"

"I haven't done anything. I was trying to let him know that the whole neighborhood could see his ass." I slump back against the cushions, a little dizzy at the memory of his firm backside. I chew on my lip.

"Uh-huh." Lucy's grinning again. "And his response to

your suggestion?"

"I think he was teasing me."

"Was this through text?"

"Yeah." I cock my head. "Why?"

"Send me a screenshot of the messages."

I shake my head as I exit out of the call, pausing her video while I search for Ben's texts. I screenshot the conversation and send it to her before connecting the video again.

"Sent."

"Okay, got it. Give me a minute." Lucy pauses her video, and I hear her muttering as she reads what I just sent her. "Well, damn. You're right." She connects the video again. "He was totally teasing you."

"Yeah, but then why the sudden one-eighty?" I pout.

"That I don't know." She scratches her head. "Maybe he's one of those commitment-phobes? Has he talked to you since?"

"I sent him a message yesterday, but he said he was busy. So, I gave him some space. He's trying to work from home, and I'm sure that's stressful." I shrug and try not to be discouraged by his dismissal.

"Sweet, summer child." Lucy shakes her head. "This guy wants you. That's obvious. But I don't get why he's so quick to push you away. Unless he's married or something."

"He's not. I never see anyone in the apartment besides him."

Lucy's brow shoots up. "You've taken up stalking now too. Aww, what a cute pair you make."

"Knock it off. I am not stalking him." Guilt creeps into my gut and twists into a gnarled knot. "Okay, maybe a little bit, but come on, it's lockdown. I can't be the only one distracted by my neighbors."

"Neighbor. Singular." Lucy laughs. "This is like some kind of rom-com chick flick. I'll make some popcorn and wait it out. And don't censor the good stuff either." She winks.

"You're twisted, you know that?"

She smiles sweetly. "It's one of my many charms."

"If you say so." I pause, searching for the right way to ask for advice. "What do I do?"

Lucy sighs. "Just be your sweet, sunshiny, annoyingly optimistic self. I'm sure it'll all work out."

"You think?" A sprout of hope takes root in my soul.

"Look, girl. If he can't see how wonderful you are, then fuck him." She squeezes her eyes closed when she realizes what she just said. "You know what I mean."

"Yeah." I chuckle, even though the words FUCK HIM have triggered a surge of heat through my whole body. "I got it."

"Anyway, I gotta run. Joey needs me to swing by the precinct before I head to work. Those masks ready yet?"

"Almost. I'm gonna finish them up tonight."

"Good, we need them." Lucy waves. "Love you! Behave."

"Always, Mom. Love you, too." I disconnect the call and stare at the hanging ivy draped across the window.

I tear myself away from thoughts of Ben and his cryptic messages. The house needs cleaning, and I have to finish those masks. I jump to my feet and grab my supplies from the cabinet.

A knock at the door makes me spin around and drop the spray bottle in my hand. "Shit." I snatch it up as the nozzle leaks on the tile.

"Just a minute." I drop a rag on the spot and place the spray bottle in the bucket before running to the door.

Mr. Donovan stands on the welcome mat with a surgical mask covering his mouth and nose. Concern for the older gentleman overwhelms me.

"Mr. Donovan, hi. Are you sick?"

"Oh, I'm fine. Just a bit of a cough." He clears his throat, and my heart constricts. The poor man.

"Is it the…" I begin, but he cuts me off.

"No, no. I've had this stubborn cough for a while now."

"Well, do you need anything? Can I help you somehow?"

He shakes his head. "No, no. My wife is taking good care of me. Too good, honestly. I had to get out of the house to keep her from fussing over me." He chuckles and coughs a few times.

"Would you like some tea?" I offer, knowing he won't accept, but I feel helpless and it bothers me.

"No, no, dear. I'll be fine. I didn't want to worry you." His eyes sparkle, and I know he's smiling. "This came for you yesterday evening while you were out. Myrtle signed for it."

"Oh, it's the fabric I ordered. I'm making cloth masks." I take the box from his hands and set it down inside. "One moment, I have something for you."

I run into the sewing room and return with a handful of masks: some with floral patterns and others with a skyline of New York print. I hand them to Mr. Donovan. "Here, I made these for you and your wife."

He cradles the gift in his trembling hands. "Thank you, Miss Weiss. This is quite thoughtful of you."

"Call me Penelope. And don't mention it." My heart surges with affection for this sweet man and his wife who helped me after my grandparents' death.

"Albert." Tears pool in his eyes, and he wipes them away with the pad of his thumb. "Once this whole lockdown is over, we would love to have you over for supper."

I laugh. "I would love that. Thank you." Joy fills me. "Oh, and if you need anything, please let me know."

"Will do." He backs away with a wave. "Enjoy your day, Penelope."

"You too, Albert." I wait until he's halfway down the steps before closing the door.

My heart aches at the conflicting emotions surging through me. I can't seem to focus through the onslaught of emotions, so I do what I always do when I need a distraction from overthinking. I clean and listen to my jams.

CHAPTER NINE
BREAKING THE LAW

BEN

LOCKDOWN DAY 18

"Yes, sir. I understand, sir." I grind my teeth and refrain from throwing the phone that's pressed to my ear.

"I understand this puts you in an uncomfortable position, but, unfortunately, the board will not consent to go through with the acquisition of your company without having the complete quarterly financial records for the past ten years." Mr. Kennedy's voice is calm and composed.

"Is it possible to postpone the deadline for another month? I'm sure this lockdown will be lifted soon. I can ensure the files are sent as soon as I have access to my office network."

"I'm sorry, son. The board was very clear in their direction with this merger." He pauses with a heavy exhale. "You have until the end of the week to get those documents to my office."

"Yes, sir." I clear my throat. "I'll take care of it. You can count on me."

"If you have any issues, contact me directly."

"Thank you. Have a good evening, sir." I hang up the phone in a daze.

What the hell am I going to do? I've exhausted every possible avenue, except breaking lockdown protocol. It seems like I have no choice now. I need that laptop to access the network. No one else had the forethought to take their work computers home with them before the lockdown. I pinch the bridge of my nose and close my eyes.

If I get caught, I'm fucked. My stomach growls. Shit, it's seven already? I grab the leftover food in the fridge and heat it. After the past few days, my determination to avoid takeout went out the window. Although I did finally order a treadmill yesterday. If anything, I can get back into my running routine, as long as this whole merger disaster doesn't throw me into a total state of misery.

I collapse into the chair and stare at my lukewarm plate of lo mein and ginger chicken. Damn it. I pick at the food, barely tasting it. If I don't eat, I'll be starving by midnight. With a grunt of annoyance, I finish the plate and clean up.

Ping. I wipe the dishwater from my hands before pulling the phone from my pocket.

Hey, Ben. Want to watch a movie?

I can't help but smile. I realize it's the first time I've smiled in days.

Three days since the last text from her. I'm an ass for ignoring her. There were a few moments where I reached for the phone to send her a quick message. But I couldn't do it.

Right now?

I can't ignore her any longer. Truth is, I don't want to, but I'm really not in the mood for chitchat.

Yeah, I mean, unless you're busy.

I'm not great company at the moment.

Aww. I'm sure that's not true.

It is. I'm a miserable fucker right now, and no one needs to see that.

*Why are you so miserable? Is there any way I can cheer you up? *Smiley Emoji**

I can think of a few ways she can cheer me up. Most of them are indecent for polite conversation, which is why I bite back the wicked thoughts of her on her knees at my feet. I rake my hand through my hair, pulling it. The sting of pain jerks me back to reality. She's trying to be a decent human being, and I'm acting like a misanthropic, horny lush.

I have a huge business deal coming up next month. Unfortunately, the files I need are in my office.

Oh, well, I'm sure you can go pick them up.

I tried. A cop stopped me a few blocks from my apartment and told me to go home and stay there.

Damn. That sucks. Is there anyone who can get them for you?

No. I already tried bribing half my staff to go get them. None are willing to face a fine or jail time for breaking lockdown.

Are you willing to?

I blink at the screen. She has a point. If I'm not willing to do it, why should I ask my employees to risk it?

You're right. I'm going to go get my papers. If I get caught, I'll just pay the fine.

I can't condone you breaking the law, but we do what we need to do, right?

I guess. Thanks.

Of course. What are friends for?

I watch the dots play on the screen as I think of a response. Friends? I guess we are. I want more than friendship, but I'll settle for what I have at the moment. Before I can reply, she sends another message.

Where's your office?

Myrtle Ave.

Is that near the hospital?

Yeah, why?

I have an idea. Do you have a car?

Not in the city.

Damn. Okay. Meet me in the alley in an hour.

I'm completely confused. What's happening? What is she planning to do? My conscience balks at the thought of involving her in this whole mess.

Why?

Just trust me. I got this.

I shake my head at the huge thumbs-up emoji she sent. This woman is full of surprises.

Then it hits me. In an hour, we will meet in person for the first time. Well, aside from the encounter outside the market, but I hardly count that as our first meeting since we barely exchanged two words. But this…this will be different.

A thrill shoots through me. I never thought I would be so fucking ecstatic to be in another person's company. I race down the hall and jump in the shower. There is no way in hell I'm meeting her smelling like a grizzled hermit with greasy hair.

Halfway through my shower, I begin to question this plan. This is a bad idea. I can't risk us both getting caught. I'm not worried about the virus. I have no problem keeping my distance from people on the street. Fuck, I'll even wear a mask. If it means I can spend time with her, it's worth the risk.

I'm a selfish bastard. I want to see her. I need those files. If I can have both, then I'm not going to examine this opportunity too closely. I can't.

Forty-five minutes later, I'm tying my running shoes. I grab my black running jacket before hazarding a glimpse of myself in the mirror. I cringe. My hair is a shaggy mess, still damp and tousled from my shower. I need a haircut. I shaved whatever scruff I'd let accumulate over the past few days, leaving the goatee.

This isn't a date. It's two friends breaking the rules. I squeeze my eyes closed and ignore the warning bells clanging desperately in the back of my mind.

I take the elevator down and slip out the back door of the building. There's no one outside. I breathe deep a few times to calm my racing heart before stepping around the dumpsters to enter the alley. Her building has an entrance just near the back of the alley, and the door is wide open, light spilling out into the darkness. As I approach, I nearly trip over a box outside the door.

When I look up, she's there with a huge box in her arms. The mask she's wearing only emphasizes her beautiful eyes. Her hair is tucked up in a neat ponytail with soft tendrils pulling free and framing her face.

"Hi." Her eyes sparkle. I can't see her mouth, but I know she's smiling. She's even prettier in person. Fuck.

"Hi." I flex my hands a few times before I reach for the box in her arms. "Let me help you with that."

"Thanks." She shifts the box into my open arms. It's heavier than it looks.

I clear my throat. "What's in here?"

"Oh, these are the masks I sewed."

I stare at her. "Uh, I'm confused."

She laughs. "Your office is near the hospital, right? Brooklyn Medical?"

I nod.

"Well, my best friend is a nurse at Brooklyn Medical, and she's working tonight. I told her I'd drop off these masks for her." She winks. "But I don't have a car. The cabs aren't running. And I can't carry them all by myself." She blinks up at me, and I swear it's like the sky has opened and sunshine is pouring from the heavens.

I can't help but be impressed. "You come up with this plan all by yourself?"

"I did." She props her hands on her ample hips. "Clever, huh?"

"Masterful." I chuckle. "And it makes me feel like less of a selfish asshole for breaking lockdown."

"Exactly. Why not water both plants at the same time?"

I shake my head. This woman is amazing. "Thank you."

"Don't thank me yet. Let's get moving. I told Lucy we would be there by nine."

"Let's go then."

"Oh wait." She reaches into her pocket and pulls out a handmade mask.

I stop breathing when she steps closer and loops the elastic over my ear, drapes the fabric across my face, and secures the opposite elastic band on my other ear. She tugs it down and secures the metal wire nosepiece before dropping her hand.

"There. Now you're ready." I'm not sure if she's whispering or breathless. I hope the latter, because I'm struggling to breathe with her being so close to me.

"Thanks." I choke on the word and pray I don't sound like a total idiot. "Shall we go?"

"Yeah."

"I'll let you lead since this is your plan."

"Okay." She closes the side door and hefts the other box into her arms. "Oh, and if anyone stops us, we're dating and living together. Got it?" She doesn't wait for an answer and forges ahead down the alley with determination.

I stare after her, blood rushing straight to my cock. Dating? Living together? The images alone are enough to make my mind implode. Oh, this is a very bad idea. But I can't bring myself to give a fuck. I'm rolling with it, consequences be damned.

Penelope

Lockdown Day 17

We make it two blocks before stopping for a quick rest. He sets the box on the bench beside mine. We're about eight blocks from the hospital. I glance at my watch.

"We're good on time."

He nods to the box. "You okay carrying that?"

I laugh and wave my hand. "Yeah, no sweat. Couldn't have carried both, though."

The streets are empty. We passed one old gentleman, wearing a blue bandana across his face like a Wild West bandit, as he walked his dog. There's almost no traffic. That's not a bad thing. But it's not a great thing either, if the cops cruise by and stop us. I'm confident in my plan, so I ignore the prickling unease.

"Let's go." I heft the box up and take the lead once more.

He's two steps behind me. I can't tell if my heart is thundering because I'm carrying a twenty-pound box of masks and walking multiple city blocks after being cooped up for a few weeks. Or, it could just be Ben. I have a feeling it's a blend of the two. My mask suddenly feels too tight, like it's suffocating me.

They're made with two layers of cotton, but they might as well be made of heavy wool the way I'm huffing and puffing. Oh, god. Okay. Calm down. Breathe slow and steady.

"These masks are nice, but they make it hard to breathe." I toss casually over my shoulder.

He comes alongside me. "Yeah, they are."

I cast a sidelong glance at his profile. He looks almost rakish with his dark hair in waves across his forehead and the mask covering what I know are the most sinfully full lips I've ever seen on a man. My hands tingle at the memory of his silky hair brushing against my fingertips when I put the mask on him.

He catches me staring, and his brown eyes sparkle with amusement in the streetlight.

I quicken my pace, knowing we're on a timeline. I hate the thought of our adventure ending. But we have a mission, and I'm a woman of my word.

After twenty minutes, we round the corner onto Myrtle Avenue.

"My building is just up here." He quickens his pace.

We stop in front of a five-story building, just across from the park. The hospital is on the other side of the trees. I can see the lights from here. After a quick struggle with the box in his arms, he manages to open the door, and we slip inside.

He sets the box on the floor and pulls the mask off, stuffing it into his pocket. "Set the box here. It'll only take me a few minutes."

"I'm coming with you." I pull the mask down, so it rests under my chin.

"Okay, but stay with me."

I nod and grab a fistful of his jacket. He whips around in confusion.

"What?" I grin. "You said to stay close."

I chuckle under my breath when I hear him mutter something strangely similar to "social distancing my ass." He deactivates the alarm system and opens the door into the main entryway.

My pace matches his, and I tighten my grip on his jacket as he leads me into the heart of the building. After climbing two flights of stairs, we arrive in front of a door, leading to Solus Incorporated.

"You work here?" My gaze skims over the open cubicles and the closed doors of the offices lining the outside walls.

"Yes." He weaves through the maze and stops in front of a large door in the front of the building.

I catch the name on the door as we enter the office he just unlocked. *Ben Statler, CEO.* I release his jacket and stare at the nameplate.

"You're the CEO?" I clap my hand over my mouth after my brainless shriek.

He doesn't look up from his desk, where he's fiddling with the drawer. "Yes."

"Holy shit." I run to the window and gently prod the two dying houseplants on the ledge. A violet and a lily. "Oh, you poor things. Ben, Ben!" I turn toward him and hiss his name in agitation.

"What?" His head snaps up.

"Do you have any water bottles?"

"Check in the breakroom at the end of the hall." He returns his attention to his computer.

I sprint down the hall and find four bottles of water. In a drawer by the fridge, I find a pair of scissors. When I return to his office, I water the two plants a little, then pierce holes in the end of the bottles and stick them upside down in the soil by the roots. There, that should keep them satisfied for a week or two at least.

I murmur a few encouraging words to the flowers before turning back to Ben.

He's staring at me with a blue backpack slung over his shoulder. "Were you talking to the plants?"

"Yes." I cross my arms. "They're nearly dead. I couldn't just leave them like that."

Ben's cheeks turn red, and he drops his gaze to the floor. "I forgot about them. My secretary told me they would improve my mood."

Looks like your mood killed them, I almost snap. But I bite my tongue. Not everyone has a green thumb. I see the clock on the wall behind Ben.

"Shit! It's nearly nine. We need to get those masks to the hospital." I exit the office ahead of Ben, who stops to lock his door. After weaving through the building, we make it to the entryway where we left the boxes.

Ben sets the alarm and puts his mask on. I slide mine up, making sure it's secure before we exit the building. Within moments, we're both crossing the street with our boxes, heading for the hospital just down the street.

Nailed it. I quicken my pace once we reach the bright lights of the hospital walkway.

Ben and I walk through the main entrance and stop at the front desk.

"Hi." The mask garbles my voice, so I speak louder. "I'm here to see Lucy Mackewitz."

"Oh, you must be Penelope! She told me you'd be coming in. Let me page her." The woman points to the row of chairs by the wall. "Just have a seat, she'll be right out."

"Thanks." I grab Ben's hand and pull him toward the row of chairs. It feels good to rest for a minute after that hike. Who'd have thought lugging a box of masks across Brooklyn would be such good cardio? I chuckle and collapse into the seat.

He turns to study my face, and his whiskey eyes narrow. "Penelope, are those...penises on your mask?"

The racing of my heart stumbles, midbeat, and sputters at the way his voice lowers as he speaks. I smile, even though I know he can't see it.

"Yes! Remember, I mentioned it to you before."

He nods.

"Well, I figured it would be a good test for maintaining six feet between me and someone else. From a distance, you can't tell what the print is. It looks like a paisley pattern. But up close, you can tell it's not." I laugh. "If you can see the dicks, you're too close."

I can't tell if Ben's expression is admiration or horror. It's difficult to tell with the mask covering the bottom of his face. The dark blue galaxy pattern I chose for his mask contrasts perfectly with his pale skin. In the bright lights, I can finally see him clearly. No grainy video due to buffering. No dim streetlight shadows. No clandestine offices. He's so close. In high definition. I can count the smattering of freckles across his exposed face. I want to peel the mask off and see if they continue like constellations against his fair skin. I've never been a fan of whiskey, but I want to drown myself in his eyes. Not brown, no, a rich vibrant hue I've never seen before.

"Penelope...I..."

"PENELOPE!" A shout breaks the spell between us, and I jump to my feet.

"Lucy!" I run toward her, only to stop quickly when I realize we're supposed to be distancing ourselves. "Sorry, I forgot. I miss you."

"I miss you too!" Lucy's wearing the scrubs I got her for Christmas, Captain America shields all over the bright blue fabric, and a plain surgical mask. She's obsessed. "Thanks for bringing those masks over. Did you make me a few to match this?" She gestures to her scrubs.

"Of course. They're on top in the big box." I point to the counter where we left the boxes.

"You're a fucking lifesaver. Thanks, hon." Her eyes widen. "How the hell did you get those two boxes over here?"

"I had some help." I gesture to Ben.

Lucy's eyes narrow as she takes him in. "Who the hell is this?" She shakes her head. "Wait, let me guess. Is this Seventh-Floor-I-Don't-Believe-in-Curtains?"

Ben clears his throat and raises a brow in my direction.

I wave him off. "Yes, this is Ben Statler. He offered to give me a hand."

I can't see Lucy's face, but I can just imagine the smirk twisting her lips. "Oh, I'm sure he did."

"Lucy!"

"I can see you two threw that social distancing thing right out the window too, huh?" Lucy gestures between Ben and me.

There's barely a foot between us, and I swear it keeps shrinking every minute. His heat radiates like a black hole, drawing me toward him. I shrug.

Lucy laughs. "Oh lord. You two." She shakes her head. "Anyway, thanks for the masks. You should get home."

"Yes, Mom." I roll my eyes.

"Listen, if the cops stop you, just tell them to call Shelly at the front desk." She points at the woman they spoke to earlier. "She'll verify you delivered these masks and the time."

"Got it."

"And Penelope, go straight home. I can't vouch for you if you don't head straight home." Her eyes widen with meaning.

I blink. What the hell is she implying? Where the hell am I supposed to go? I glance at Ben, who's shifting his weight uncomfortably from one foot to the other. Oh...OOOOOOhhhhhh.

"I'll call you tomorrow." Lucy points at me and then turns to Ben. "Nice to meet you, Ben Statler. No funny business, got it?"

"I wouldn't dream of it, ma'am." He proffers a theatrical bow.

"Smartass," Lucy mutters before waving. "Behave kids. Some of us need to work."

"Bye, Lucy. Love you too."

She disappears through the automatic door, carrying a box of the masks.

Ben turns to me. "Shall we go? It'll take us less time to walk home now that we aren't carrying all that weight."

I nod and head for the door. I'm hyper-aware of Ben following behind me, and I wonder if he has any clue that Lucy just sized him up.

We step out into the chilly spring night air, and I shiver. But not from the cold.

CHAPTER TEN
WHAT'S SOCIAL DISTANCING?

BEN

LOCKDOWN DAY 18

I fall into step beside her, like a towering, but loyal, hound. Secure in the knowledge I have what I need to finalize the merger, I'm now acutely aware of the woman beside me. I glance at her from the corner of my eye. The top of her head just reaches my shoulder.

There's a pull as we walk, a companionable sway with every step that makes us drift closer until her shoulder brushes my arm. She shifts away with a laugh and apologizes. The mask hides both our reactions, and I hate them even more because of it.

We make it to Columbus Park without any issue. There's no one on the streets and very little traffic. I feel like an asshole for not sneaking to my office a week ago. But then, I wouldn't be with her like this.

"Brrr." She rubs her arms and stares at me. "You cold?"

"Not really." I stuff my hands deeper into my pockets.

"You okay?"

"Yeah, just thinking."

"Thinking about what?" She sways into me on purpose. Is she teasing me?

"How much I needed this." My admission shocks me the moment the words leave my lips.

"To get out of the house or to get your paperwork?"

"Both." I shrug. "But I meant being with you."

Her head snaps up, and she locks eyes with me. Even amid the shadows, I can see her surprise. She stops walking.

"Really?"

I turn and shrug. "Yeah." I lick my lips and frown when the mask gets in the way.

Even though this is the first time we've been in each other's physical company, it doesn't feel that way. It feels good. Liberating. Comfortable. Fan-fucking-tastic.

"I like talking to you." I ruffle my hair before shoving my hand back in my pocket.

"Could've fooled me." She huffs and walks on, shoving past me, even though she has four feet of the walkway in every direction.

"Hold up." I reach for her, but she's already beyond my grasp.

She spins around and faces me, walking backward at a brisk pace. "You've been avoiding me since our date Saturday night."

I sigh. She's not wrong. "Yeah, about that. I owe you an apology."

"Yes, you do." Penelope props her hands on her hips and spins her back to me.

I look up toward the midnight blue sky and curse. "Penelope."

She quickly crosses the street and slips into Cadman Plaza. We're not far from our respective homes. Panic strikes like a physical blow. I don't want this to end.

This woman has the oddest assortment of traits. Quirky and charming, talented and determined. Lord help me, but when she started to talk to the plants in my office, I nearly lost it. It took every ounce of my control not to laugh. She truly is a ray of sunshine. And I'm tired of living beneath a thundercloud.

I jog to catch up to her and grab her arm. "Penelope, wait."

She stills under my touch but doesn't turn. I pull my mask down and walk around to face her. Her eyes are bright with tears.

"I was an asshole."

She holds my gaze and folds her arms across her chest. "That's not an apology."

"I'm sorry, Penelope." I shift from foot to foot as she bears down on my soul with her stare. "I'm sorry for teasing you and then pushing you away."

"Why did you push me away?" She cocked her head. I wish I could see her mouth right now. I can't tell if she's smiling or not.

Anxiety makes my heart pound and my skin itch. "I don't know."

She nods.

"I'm shit at this. I suck at friendships. Evan can confirm that fact. He's known me since we were kids. I've never been in a stable relationship." I lift my hands in defeat. "I'm a miserable bastard. I pour everything into my business until there's nothing left for anyone else, and I'm all alone."

"Who's Evan?"

Leave it to her to latch onto that one detail. "My business partner."

"Oh, Ben." She sighs and shakes her head. "You're not alone."

I freeze when she wraps her arms around my waist, pinning my arms to my sides. The press of her warmth against me sends my heart into overdrive. I inhale sharply and catch the sweet scent of sugar and the tang of lemon. My eyes drift closed.

When I open them, she's staring up at me. Her lips hidden by the damned mask. I pull my arm free and tug the mask down. Her lopsided grin tips my restraint.

"This isn't very good social distancing." I choke out the words, wanting nothing more than to taste her.

"It's not social distancing. It's physical distancing." She teases me. "Get it right."

I roll my eyes. "Either way, we suck at it."

"Yes, we do." She grabs the front of my jacket in her fist.

I'm unable to resist the gravitational pull between us. She pulls me down, and I meet her halfway. The moment our lips touch, it's a supernova of sensation. I wrap my arms around her waist and lift her. She squeals against my mouth and throws her arms around my neck.

I'm lost in her. The soft slide of her lips on mine. I groan at the hint of watermelon when I lick the seam of her mouth. She opens for me and I devour her. Sweet and spicy, like early autumn. I'm smitten and it feels so fucking good.

She moans, and I'm painfully aware of the erection straining against my zipper.

"Well, well. What have we here? That doesn't look like six feet to me."

Penelope jerks from my embrace, and we both turn toward the voice behind us.

My heart slams to the pavement and splatters like roadkill.

"You'd better have a good reason for being out." The police officer shakes his head and reaches for his notepad and pen.

Shit.

Penelope

Lockdown Day 18

Holy shit! He's actually kissing me. Is this really happening? When he lifts me off the ground and deepens the kiss, I surrender whatever thoughts are floating through my mind and focus solely on Ben and his wickedly delicious mouth.

I moan and arch against him. Oh my god, is that his—

"Well, well. What have we here? That doesn't look like six feet to me."

The kiss disintegrates instantly. I scramble out of Ben's embrace at the sound of that familiar voice. Oh shit. Why couldn't I have waited until we got back to the apartment?

Why? Fuck. Of all the nights. I want to tear my hair out.

"You'd better have a good reason for being out." The cop pulls his notepad out.

He hasn't seen me yet. Shit. It's only a matter of time before he realizes it's me. I step between Ben and the cop.

"Hey, Joey."

Joey's attention snaps up. "Penny? What the hell are you doing out here? You better have a damn good reason for bein' out at this hour. Are you hurt? Do you need help? I swear to God, Lucy will never let me hear the end of it if something happened to you." His gaze lingers on me for a moment before it shifts to Ben. "Who the fuck are you?" He points to Ben. "Is he forcing himself on you, Penny?"

Ben tenses behind me. I put my hand on his thigh and squeeze. He stills beneath my touch.

"No, Joey. I'm fine. Ben helped me carry the masks I made for Lucy to the hospital. You can call her and verify that we were just there."

Joey doesn't look convinced, and his gaze narrows. "I trust you, Penny." He scowls harder. "But him. Nah, I don't trust him. He looks shady as hell."

I glance at Ben, then back at Joey. "It's all good. He's with me. I made some masks for the hospital, and he helped me carry them over. I swear."

"You two dating?"

"Yeah. Since February." I'm going to hell for lying, but I can't seem to care.

"Really? How come Lucy didn't tell me?" Joey crosses his arms over his burly chest.

"I told her not to tell you." I hate lying to him, but I know Joey's had a thing for me ever since we met in December. "I'm sorry, Joey. I should've told you."

Joey sniffs. "Yeah, well. I knew something was up when Lucy wouldn't give me your number last month and told me to find another woman to annoy."

I'm speechless. Wasn't Lucy harassing me about her brother just a few weeks ago? I shake my head. "We're just gonna head home, okay, Joey?"

He tucks the pad into his pocket and nods. "Straight home. And save the kinky shit for the bedroom, would ya?"

My face heats. "I promise. Thanks, Joey."

He waves. "I'll see ya."

I turn and grab Ben's hand. We walk in the opposite direction and cut across the street. Once I know we're out of Joey's sight, I slow my pace. Ben's still got ahold of my hand, and he pulls me closer as we walk.

"Oh, shit. I'm so sorry about that." I glance over my shoulder, just to make sure Joey isn't following us.

"I take it he's a friend of yours?" Ben's question holds a bite of jealousy.

I stare at him and squeeze his hand. "That's Lucy's brother."

"He's a cop?" Ben seems surprised by this.

"Yeah, hasn't been on the force long. He was in the Army for a bit before he joined the NYPD."

We wander up the street in silence. The city never sleeps, so it's strange for it to be this quiet. I glance at my watch, thinking it's later than it is. Ten o'clock.

Finally, we reach our street. A sense of dread settles in the pit of my stomach as our buildings rise before us. I don't want this to end. I want to finish what we started in the park.

Ben pulls me right past my doorstep and into the alley. A thrill of excitement shoots through me, and my body ignites.

"Ben, where are we going?" I pull on his hand, slowing his pace.

He turns, and my heart flutters at the heat in his slow appreciation of my body. "Why did you tell him we were dating?"

I chew on my lip and shrug.

"Do you want to go home?"

I shake my head. My heartbeat echoes in my ears, drowning the world out.

"Do you want to come with me?"

I nod, unable to trust my voice.

His smile erases whatever reservations remain. Oh, shit. How can one man be so damn handsome? His hair falls across his forehead, and he smooths it away with his free hand.

"Come on." He tugs my hand, and I follow with a ball of nervous excitement building in the pit of my stomach.

In moments, he has the back door unlocked, and we climb the stairs to the seventh floor. I nearly collapse once we reach his floor. After not having been out of the house for three weeks, I realize how weak my cardio game is. I guess those daily walks in the park were helping. My legs wobble when I walk down the hallway, forcing me to cling tighter to him.

Ben unlocks his apartment door and motions for me to enter first.

Excitement pings through me. I've always wondered what his apartment looked like. The furnishings are masculine and classy. Dark stained wood, brass accents, a rich brown leather couch, and a huge painting of a forest of aspens dominate the living space.

I wander into the kitchen and admire the clean lines. White cabinetry, stainless steel appliances, and oak hardwood flooring. My fingers caress the smooth, cool marble countertop before I place my purse on it.

Ben leans against the wall as I move from room to room taking in the layout and the décor. I purposely avoid the bedroom and return to the living room, where he's watching me with his arms folded across his broad chest.

"This place is amazing." I spin around once more in awe.

"It looks better now."

"Why? Did you just have it renovated?"

"No, because you're here."

My jaw drops, even though my heart is singing. "Ben." I wave him off.

"I'm serious. I've never had anyone over to my apartment, well besides my business partner, Evan. Up until a few weeks ago, I rarely spent any time here." He crosses the space between us and removes my mask completely. His is already gone. "I didn't realize what it was missing until this moment."

"You know that's the sweetest, but corniest, thing I've ever heard." My breath shudders when he brushes his fingertips down my jaw. His hands are fucking massive. I tip my head back and meet his gaze.

He shrugs. "It's true."

"Ben?" I grasp his open jacket with both hands. "Finish what you started in the park."

When he wraps his arms around my waist and lifts me off the ground, I yelp in surprise. He presses his lips against mine with a desperation I meet wholeheartedly. I bury my hands in his hair, reveling in his gasping moan when I tug gently.

It's been so long since I've had the warm bliss of physical contact. Too long. I miss the comfort of a friendly hug. But this, damn, it's overwhelming. I cling to him, needing to absorb his heat and scent. I want him branded on me. Even though I know I shouldn't, with all the chaos in the world and this infernal pandemic, I throw caution to the wind. Not because I want it, but because I need it. It's a deep, physical ache as real as a third-degree burn or a compound fracture. Humanity wasn't made for isolation. We crave connection. We need it for our very survival.

He rubs his nose against mine and pulls back to search my face. His smile steals my breath. "What are you thinking about?"

"Who says I'm thinking?"

"I do." He kisses me again. "Stop." Another kiss. "Thinking." His lips trail along my jaw with tiny nips tingling in their wake.

I tangle my hands in his hair as he pulls me down onto the couch with him. With my knees planted on either side of his hips, I have unrestricted access to all of him. His silky hair slides through my fingers, while his hands wander the length of my spine in a languid caress. Those huge hands play havoc on my senses. I arch against his touch, needing more. The motion moves my hips against his, and I'm immediately rewarded with the thick press of his erection against my core.

"If you keep that up, this won't last long," he whispers against my mouth, and there's something sacred about what we're doing: an ancient ritual meant to unite and bind.

"Sorry." I smirk and rock my hips against him again.

His hands grip my hips, holding me steady. He inhales sharply. "Seriously."

"Been a while for you too, huh?" I press closer, leaning my weight against his chest.

"You have no idea." He closes his eyes and takes a few measured breaths.

"Hey." I kiss his full lips gently. He opens his eyes. "Take your pants off."

The lopsided smile he gives me makes my heart tumble in a series of glitter-soaked summersaults. I scramble from his lap and peel off every article of clothing in record time. His gaze follows my movements as he stands and pulls off his pants in one smooth motion. After he kicks them aside, he hooks a hand around my waist and pulls me down onto the couch once more.

There's nothing but hard, hot man beneath me. The thought leaves me spinning, and, I'll admit, a bit breathless. He leans forward and pulls off his jacket and shirt, tossing them somewhere behind me. I laugh at the sudden change in character.

"What's funny?" His voice seems deeper. It's sinfully delicious.

"Nothing."

He thrusts his cock against my slick center, making me gasp. "Tell me."

"Your apartment is so perfect. It surprises me to see you make a mess of it." I wiggle on his lap, trying to get closer. His heat sinks into me, and I relish the sensation of skin on skin. The delicious friction of it sends my body into a crescendo.

"You think you know me so well." His hands grasp my thighs. His cock presses insistently against my opening.

I groan and wrap my arms around his neck, leaning fully into him. "I don't know much about you, honestly."

"Does it matter?"

"At the moment?" I meet his molten caramel gaze and shake my head. "No."

He grins. That wicked, teasing expression sends sparks of need like fireworks through me. "Would you rather I stopped?" He moves to push me away. "We can wait."

"Fuck no." I grasp him tighter. "Don't you dare stop now."

His laugh unleashes a hunger inside me I hadn't realized I possessed. I kiss him hard, rubbing myself against him, desperate for affection. He tilts his head to deepen the kiss, and I'm falling, hard and fast. His taste intoxicates me, his scent envelops me. I'm so fucking gone.

He lifts my hips and guides himself to my opening. I press my hand on his chest. "Wait."

He blinks at me, eyes hooded and lust-hazed. "What's wrong?"

"Do you have protection?" I murmur the words, afraid it'll shatter the spell between us.

"Shit." He presses his forehead to mine. "I'm sorry. It's been so long."

I chuckle and palm his cheek in my hand, forcing him to look at me. "Give me a minute."

I slide off his lap and grab my bag on the counter. After a moment of sifting through the contents, I find a box of condoms I had stashed inside. I open it and pull one out.

Ben waits completely naked with a prominent erection. His lips twist in a smirk. "Were you planning on having sex with me tonight?"

"No." I saunter back to him with the packet between my fingers. "But I came prepared." I rip the foil packet with my teeth and slip the condom out. With great care, I make a show of leaning forward and rolling it onto him.

The heat in his gaze could ignite a bonfire. He gasps with every brush of my fingertips.

"Tease." He grabs me by the waist and pulls me on top of him again.

There's no preamble, no foreplay, no romantic gesture. He presses into me, and I sink onto his length with a long moan. He fills me completely and then some. I didn't think I could feel this full, this complete. My fingers dig into his shoulders and his into my hips.

"Holy shit." His words echo deep in my soul, and I nod in reply.

When he moves inside me, he pulls me against him and kisses me hard. The rhythm increases as the need intensifies. I rock my hips, giving and taking, while he reciprocates. Our kisses become a frenzied mixture of panting and tasting, of teeth and tongue.

He urges me faster. I cling to him. My head drops to his shoulder, and I graze my teeth against his pale skin. He hisses.

"Do it. Mark me." His words are like fuel to the raging fire consuming me.

I trail bites along his shoulder and neck, careful not to break skin.

"Fuck, yes." He slips his hand between us.

When his finger circles my clit, I buck my hips hard and moan. "More." I quicken my pace, needing to chase the orgasm hovering just out of reach.

Ben urges me on. His teeth leave gentle sensitive bites along my neck. My body spirals into a tight ball until the tension explodes. The sensations course through me, wave after wave of energy, pulsing and reeling, leaving me blissfully shaken.

My body pulses around him, until he finally loses control. He buries his head in my neck, panting and swearing as he comes. I smile at the wreckage of our passion. Slick with sweat, we nestle closer. His grip tightens.

I sigh. Contentment settles over me, and I can't stop

myself from chuckling.

"What's funny now?" His voice reverberates through me.

"Us." I pull back, so I can read his expression. He's blissfully sated with those glazed-over whiskey eyes and a lopsided grin. I brush the lock of hair from his eyes.

"Us what?" His gaze narrows.

"We're really bad at this social distancing thing."

"Fuck social distancing." He hugs me tighter.

My heart swells with affection for this strangely endearing man. "Aww, Ben, you're such a romantic."

He grunts and closes his eyes. I kiss his soft lips. "Come on, handsome. Take me to bed."

When he finally pulls himself together, he leads me to his bedroom, where he spends the rest of the night trying to convince me he's not against social distancing, but he has no intention of letting any space between us any time soon.

Who am I to argue with his logic?

CHAPTER ELEVEN
DON'T DO IT, MAN.

BEN

LOCKDOWN DAY 19

Waking up is hard. At least that's what it feels like today. I stretch, but there's a lot less space in my king-sized bed this morning. My leg brushes something warm beside me. I reach for it, wanting to soak it in, and drift back to sleep. Without hesitation, I wrap my arms around it and draw it against me, nestling into the soft heat. It's heaven.

A soft moan pulls me from dreamland. I crack my eyes open. A tangle of dark hair and pale skin blurs my vision. I pull back a bit and realize I'm not alone. *Penelope.*

My grip tightens around her. I can't remember the last time I shared my bed with anyone. Literally. I expect annoyance or irritation to bombard me, but it never comes. A still, sweet ache settles in my chest, and I moan at the hum of contentment. She presses against the full length of me. Our legs lay entwined, her hand grasps my forearm, where it rests against her side.

I'm afraid if I move, I'll wake her. I don't want to fall asleep again. I want to enjoy the moment and memorize her scent, her touch. She fits perfectly right where she is.

The thought has my mind spinning a hundred miles per hour. I barely know her, and yet, I wouldn't trade this moment for all the success in the world. New and strange as it is, I want it. I'm desperate for it.

I smile, and her hair brushes my nose when she arches back against me. If someone would have told me how yesterday was going to end, I would have laughed in their face. This, whatever it is, shouldn't feel as good as it does. I can't complain because it's become as necessary as breathing.

She rubs against me like a cat stirring from an afternoon nap in the sunshine. I shift and allow her to roll in my embrace. Her hazel eyes seem greener in the morning light. She yawns and gives me a lazy smile.

"Morning." Her sleep-laced voice has my cock at full attention.

"Morning." I ignore the urge to roll her onto her back and drive into her. "Did you sleep well?"

She reaches up and brushes her hair away from her face. "Mmmhmmm." The murmur and nod combination only intensify the cute factor of the woman in my bed. "What about you?"

I stretch and slide my arm around her, pulling her against me. "I haven't slept that good in a long time." The admission soothes the agitation that has been simmering beneath my skin for the last few weeks.

Penelope nestles against my side. The brush of her bare skin against mine has my body begging for an encore. After the couch, we took it to the bedroom, where I explored every glorious inch of her before taking her again. Was it possible to get drunk from physical contact? Touch drunk. Is that a thing? It must be. I've never crashed so hard, so fast, let alone slept so deeply.

I trace my fingers across her bare shoulder, lost in thought when she nudges me.

"What are you thinking about?" Her breath whispers across my chest.

"Touch drunk." The words spill from my mouth, and I sound delusional.

She props herself up. A furrow forms between her brows as she searches my face. "Touch drunk?" She laughs, and it's the pure delight pouring over me.

I grin back. "What?" I shake my head. "You asked."

Her laughter subsides. "Sorry. I did. But I've never heard

of such a thing."

Truth is, I haven't either, but I can't take it back now. I shrug. "It makes sense though, doesn't it?"

"Being touch drunk?" She bites her lower lip in thought. "Not really. Explain it to me."

I admire the soft curve of her cheek and the full swell of her lips before I reply. Damn, she's beautiful. How the hell did I get here? What did I do to deserve this ray of sweet, refreshing sunshine?

"Ben." She nudges me again.

"Oh, sorry." I clear my throat and focus on her hazel eyes. "You were a hugger, before all this lockdown, social-distancing shit, weren't you?"

She blinks, and a slow smile spreads across her face. "Yeah, I guess I was."

"Do you miss it? The small interactions, hugs, handshakes, high-fives, intimate conversations, you know, the stuff we all took for granted before this mess?"

"Yes." She nods and drops her gaze quickly. I immediately regret my words. Fuck.

"Hey." I tilt her chin up with my fingers. Tears spill over her cheeks. "I'm sorry. I didn't mean to upset you."

"You didn't." She sniffs and wipes the tears away. "Sorry, I mean. It's been building for a while, I think." She shakes her head, as though trying to rid herself of the darkness crowding her mind. "I get it now. The touch drunk thing."

"Yeah?"

She nods. "After not having physical contact for so long, you forget how important it is. How much you miss it."

I cup her cheek in my hand, and her eyes drift closed.

"When you get it, it overwhelms you. Intoxicates you." She opens her eyes and holds my gaze.

The breath I'm holding whooshes from my lungs when she leans down and kisses my forehead. Without hesitation, I wrap my arms around her waist and roll her beneath me.

A gasp of surprise leads to a moan of pleasure I steal

from her lips in a heady kiss. She buries her hands in my hair. I wedge myself between her thighs and find her wet and willing.

"Ben." She arches against me.

I love hearing her breathless voice whisper my name. I press against her slick opening. "Shit."

"Aren't you forgetting something?"

I remove myself long enough to grab a condom and put it on. Then, I'm right back where I was, pushing into her. Her eyes flutter closed, and I'm mesmerized by the flush of color rising in her cheeks when I move my hips. She tightens around me, and I'm lost.

We cling to each other, both desperate to chase the pleasure of the moment. But it's more than that. It's deeper, more visceral, and I'm afraid we both feel it.

"Stop thinking." She smooths her hand across my forehead and cups my cheek. Her gaze burns straight to my soul. "Yes. More Ben. Take what you need."

I quicken my pace. Her words spark some primal drive, lingering in my subconscious.

Penelope gasps and slips her hand between us. When she circles her clit, her body tightens around me. I barely cling to any coherent thought as we ride out the storm together. Within moments, her climax sends her into a boneless bliss. She moans and I'm captivated by the sight of her flushed cheeks and glazed expression.

My orgasm rushes through me in an instant, hurtling like a bullet through the air. When it strikes its target, I'm spent, both physically and emotionally.

I ease back so I don't crush her. She's grinning. "What?"

"A girl could get used to this." Her eyes twinkle as she shifts beneath my weight.

So could I. The thought flies through my head quickly, but I push it away. We're already going at the speed of light with this relationship. The last thing I want to do is make a stupid mistake by rushing into anything more complicated. A small voice in the back of my mind is screaming at me, mocking me. *Idiot. You're already in over your head.*

Startled by the uninvited thoughts crowding my mind, I collapse onto the bed beside her. If I chase that dreamy look in her eyes, I'll drown. Panic starts to creep into my mind. What the hell? I shove my hand through my hair.

"Hey." Penelope hovers over me. "You okay?"

I steel myself for the sweet ache radiating through my chest at the sight of her when I meet her concerned gaze. Fuck. It stings. I can't do it. I close my eyes and inhale deeply.

"What just happened?" Her voice has an edge to it. She's hurt, and I feel like a total ass. But I can't stop the brick wall from appearing between us.

"Nothing."

"Bullshit." Her fingertips burn my jaw. "Look at me."

I sigh and mask all emotions before opening my eyes.

She searches my face for a silent moment. Hurt and uncertainty mingle with the pleasured flush of her skin.

The sting of regret stabs me through the heart. Apologize. Explain. Something. Don't push her away. But I can't open my mouth. I'm paralyzed, trapped inside my own mind. Fuck.

For a moment, I'm convinced there are fresh tears on the horizon. I brace myself. But they never come. In a blink, her eyes clear, and she nods.

"I should go."

Part of my soul dies at those words. *Stop her, moron.*

She slides away, and the rest of my soul shrivels into an empty husk. I cringe as she disappears into the bathroom, carrying her clothes. The door clicks and locks, and it's like the air's been sucked from the room. I can't breathe.

I lay there surrounded by the scent of her, of us. I replay it over and over, wondering how I can untangle it and put it back together. I fucked up, and I know it. But the truth terrifies me. I'm not ready to face it. Will I ever be?

The door opens, and I'm struck stupid. She looks the same as she did last night. Only this time, she's not smiling.

Go to her. Tell her you were an asshole. Beg forgiveness. Grovel if you have to, just don't let her leave. I tell the voice raging in my mind to shut up. But it persists, badgering me as she grabs her condoms on the nightstand. I don't move. I can't. I'm such an idiot.

"I don't know what happened, Ben." Penelope sighs, and it takes all my effort not to break in two. "But if you want to talk, you know where to find me." Without another word, she leaves.

I lay in bed and listen to the rustle in the living room as she gathers her things. The sound of the front door closing pushes me into the cavernous abyss I've been standing over. Shit. Shit. Shit.

I can't deal with this. Not now. No. The only person who showed me any kindness during this whole fiasco, I just used and hurt. And now I feel like the world's biggest ass. Fuck, I can't do this.

When I finally climb from the bed, I deposit the sordid reminder of my actions into the trash and take a shower. I have work to do. I need to focus on that.

Yet even as I dive into the files and start compiling information for Mr. Kennedy's request, she haunts me. I fucked up, and I know it. But I can't bring myself to acknowledge the truth because I'm an asshole who can't navigate a meaningful relationship.

I'm in love with Penelope, and I don't know what the fuck to do with this information. So I do what I do best. I push it away.

PENELOPE

LOCKDOWN DAY 19

The persistent ringing wakes me. My head aches. Congestion makes it pound, but it's more than that. Ben's face flashes to the forefront of my mind and fresh tears form in the corners of my eyes. I blink them away. No. No more tears.

The phone stops ringing. I roll over, grab it from the nightstand, and turn the ringer on silent. I don't even check to see who's called me, even though I want to know. If it's anyone but Ben, I'll be disappointed.

I snort and roll over, burying my face in the downy comforter. Disappointment seems to be a common side effect of the pandemic, aside from the virus itself.

Once I left Ben's apartment, I held it together until I reached my brownstone. Halfway inside the door, I fell apart. Memories flooded me. Everything. Memories of my grandparents greeting me at the door and wrapping me in warm hugs. Grandma and I making cookies in the kitchen. Grandpa doing puzzles at the dining room table and reading the paper in his recliner.

A dam burst open, and emotions I hadn't even realized I'd been harboring came crashing down like a tsunami, pulling my feet from under me. I wandered through the house with a box of tissues under my arm, tears pouring down my face, sniffling and mumbling under my breath how much I missed them.

Hours later, once I calmed down, I made my way to the roof to check on my plants, which only triggered another wave of fresh tears. I tried to ignore the pull of the neighboring building. But my gaze continued to drift to the seventh-floor windows, searching for a glimpse of him. My body hummed at the thought of Ben, even though my mind raged in anger and disappointment at his dismissal. What did I do? What have I done?

I finished caring for my garden and retreated to the comfort of my bed. I cried until exhaustion pulled me under.

The clock on the nightstand flashes 6:07 pm. I groan. What is wrong with me? A whole day wasted. But even the knowledge that this is unusual for me isn't motivation enough to get my ass out of bed. No. The grief finally found me at my lowest point and wrapped me in its heavy embrace. I let it pull me down and purge whatever remained.

Still, disappointment lingers like smudged fingerprints on the windowpane. It dulls my view, blurring my reality.

I don't even know how many days we've been under lockdown. I didn't pay attention. Until this moment, I didn't care. I focused on every day as it came. But now, it feels like eighty years have passed since I've had the pleasure of companionship. A friend for dinner, a trip to the movies, a walk in the park, a hug from my grandmother…my heart lurches at the dark void forming around it.

"No." I ground out and punch the pillow beside me. "No, I won't let this consume me." With a groan, I sit up. My body protests at the motion, and I heat at the reminder of what Ben and I shared.

I close my eyes, unable to fight any longer. Snapshots flash in my mind. Ben beneath me. Ben over me. Ben holding me. Ben kissing me. Ben making love to me.

"Shit." I drop my pounding head into my hands as if trying to stop the onslaught. "Ben, why?"

Why did he push me away after what we shared? I saw the moment he shut himself away. Lucy always told me I was more perceptive than any person should be. Then she would tell me to mind my own goddamn business. But with Ben, I didn't even try to peel back the layers.

Over the last couple of weeks, something blossomed between us, something I tried not to over-analyze. We were both lonely and found a connection. Why was that wrong? Yes, the fact that we bonded so quickly seemed unusual, but what was normal about our circumstances? Not a damn thing.

I shake my head and slowly climb to my feet. I want tea. Tea sounds really good. The kitchen is dark when I pad into the room. As I go through the process of prepping the kettle and getting out my favorite mug, my thoughts return to Ben.

The thrill of being able to help both Ben and Lucy yesterday would have been enough. But I never anticipated my reaction to Ben once we physically occupied the same space. Like, I knew how handsome he was and the sexy lilt of his voice. I expected those things to affect me. His presence, all six foot something, overpowered any resemblance of restraint. I wanted him the moment he appeared in the alley. Any rational person would have run back inside and called the whole thing off.

I'm not saying I was irrational. No, it was more like we were two souls floating aimlessly in space. When we crossed each other's paths, our worlds became linked. Why fight the gravitational pull of fate? Contrary to my earlier breakdown, I believe everything happens for a reason. Even though I can't see it now, there's a reason for Ben and I meeting, sharing a romantic connection, and him pushing me away. The last piece of that hurts like hell. I won't lie.

The kettle whistles and I pull it from the heat. Maybe we just needed to blow off some steam? The thought makes me laugh. Crazy how my mind connects things. Maybe we just needed something to help us get through the moment? Another surge of disappointment rips through me.

It sure doesn't feel that way. It felt like a whole lot more than just two strangers using their chemistry to purge some sexual tension. I sigh and pour the hot water into the mug.

There's not a whole lot I can do about it, not until he decides to reach out. When I asked him to talk to me, I could see it right there in his eyes. The flash of uncertainty, fear, and vulnerability before it vanished behind a well-constructed mask of indifference. For all his tough, no-bullshit exterior, Ben is a sensitive man, desperate for connection.

Touch drunk. I smile at his words. Only a man who didn't understand the necessity of physical contact would use such an analogy. I knew exactly what he meant. I felt it too. I think I felt a whole lot more than that, but it seemed too soon for such sentiments.

I smile at a picture of my grandparents on the mantle, next to a row of potted violets. Grandma and Grandpa had known each other for all of a week before he proposed. Granted, times were different, but love doesn't alter that much, does it? When you know, you know, right?

I blow on the hot beverage before taking a sip. It warms me down to my toes. "What do you think, Grams? Am I crazy?" I sip the tea again. "I must be if I'm talking to myself."

The tea fortifies me. I sort through some mail on the table as I drink the tea and debate what to make for supper. Maybe I'll just order out tonight? I haven't eaten all day, but I'm not as hungry as I should be.

"I'll just order something from Mario's." I pull my phone from my pocket and unlock it.

Four missed calls and ten text messages. Two of the calls are from Lucy as well as all ten text messages. The other two calls are from Mr. Donovan. I return his call.

"Hello?" The woman's voice on the other line is unexpected.

"Hi, this is Penelope Weiss. I live in the brownstone beside Mr. and Mrs. Donovan. I saw I missed a call from their number. This number."

"Oh, yes, Ms. Weiss. Mr. Donovan is my father. I'm Eugenia."

"Call me Penelope. Is everything okay?"

"Well, no. My father isn't doing well."

"I'm sorry to hear that. Where is he? Does he have the virus?" I feel sick to my stomach.

"He's home now, but we've had a home care nurse come and assess him. She's not convinced he has the virus, given his prior history."

"Prior history?" I shake my head. "I'm sorry, I don't mean to pry. I mean your father spoke to me yesterday, and he assured me it was a persistent cough. I'm just worried about him."

"Thank you for your concern." Eugenia paused. "Dad was diagnosed with emphysema last year. We've been working on treatments for it."

"I'm sorry. I didn't know." Concern weighs heavy on my shoulders.

"Don't worry. Dad doesn't want people to fuss over him. He's convinced he's going to die when he's damn well good and ready." She chuckles. "Anyway, I wanted to let you know. He's been tested, but they're recommending we quarantine and contact anyone he's interacted with, just in case."

A sad dread hits the pit of my stomach like a concrete block sinking to the bottom of the Hudson. "Thanks for letting me know. I appreciate it."

"Of course. I'll call you once I hear from the nurse about his results. Dad's waving at me telling me to stop making you worry. He says he's fine."

I smile at the thought of Mr. Donovan getting indignant. "Well, he's practically family, so I'm allowed to worry about him. Let me know if you need anything. I make a delicious chicken noodle soup."

"I may take you up on it. Mom is on a cleaning spree and has left all the cooking to me." She sighs. "I guess we're all stuck together for a couple of weeks."

"I'm glad they have you." I send my best wishes and end the conversation on a false note of cheer.

I finish my tea and put the cup in the sink. My reflection in the window makes me pause.

"The world has gone mad." I shake my head and retreat to the bathroom.

After the incident with Ben and my emotional breakdown this afternoon, the news of Mr. Donovan's illness effectively kills any appetite I have. My phone vibrates in my pocket again. Lucy, probably.

I open her texts and scan them.

Are you at Ben's?

Joey told me about you and Ben crawling all over each other in the park.

Did you spend the night at his place?

Where are you?

Answer the goddamn phone.

Are you ignoring me?

This isn't like you.

You're lucky I have to work in an hour.

You better not be dead in an alley somewhere.

Don't make me send Joey over to do a welfare check.

Please respond. I need to know you're okay.

The last one pulls at my conscience. I type out a response. *I'm fine. I'm at home. I'll tell you about it tomorrow. It's been a rough day. Love you. Be safe.* I hit send and close messenger.

I want to text Ben. My finger hovers over the icon. Damn it. I toss the phone on the bed and head into the shower. I can't do it. If he wants to talk to me, he knows how to pick up the phone.

I hesitate in the doorway and glance back at the phone. I do need to tell him about Mr. Donovan, even though they don't think he has the virus. We didn't maintain any kind of distance, social or physical, last night. It's the only responsible thing to do.

I quickly type out a simple explanation and hit send before I add something like *I miss you* or *I think I love you.*

Under the hot spray of the shower, the truth sinks beneath my skin and saturates my soul. I'm in love with Ben, and it hurts too much to think he may not love me back.

CHAPTER TWELVE
DUMBASS

BEN

LOCKDOWN DAY 23

The rich scent of coffee fills the apartment. But even the strongest Sumatra can't shake me from the grip of exhaustion. Every night since Penelope walked out that door has left me adrift. Sleep alludes me, night after night. Caffeine and nicotine have done nothing to ease the debilitating edge of insomnia.

I retreated into work. Three days spent sorting through financial documents and organizing them into a coherent, presentable PDF. Mr. Kennedy made his request crystal clear. I sent the file via Dropbox at midnight on Saturday. It's Monday morning, and I haven't heard anything from Mr. Kennedy or his associates.

My inbox is overflowing. I began sorting it yesterday and barely made a dent. Today, I fully intend to finish the job, if the coffee can keep me awake long enough. I want to crawl back into bed and sleep for a week, but I know that won't happen. Lying in that bed only reminds me of Penelope. My gaze drifts toward the couch. Fuck, the apartment is tainted by her presence.

The last message from her was to let me know about her neighbor being sick and it possibly being the virus that has the whole world twisted up with fear and uncertainty. She'd been in contact with him and then with me. Sweet of her to let me know, but the cold, impersonal message left me wondering if I'd fucked things up beyond salvation. I never replied. *Shit, I need a distraction.*

Maybe I should run. The treadmill I ordered last week arrived on Friday afternoon. It sits in the box in the corner of the room. My brain alternates between work and the promise of a runner's high. Neither will fully distract me from her. I hang my head in disgust. I can't escape her, no matter what I do.

I rake my hand through my hair and focus on the computer screen. Work until noon, then put the treadmill together. A run sounds like the perfect cure for that mid-afternoon slump.

Ten minutes into purging the inbox, my phone rings. I pick it up. "Evan. Why am I not surprised to have you crawl out from whatever rock you're hiding under once the work is done?"

"Well, hello to you too, sunshine." Evan's voice grates against my last nerve. Damn optimist, which is the main reason I've been avoiding his calls, but with the merger looming, we need to be on the same page. I wish he was here, so I could strangle him for leaving me to deal with this mess alone.

"Are you still in the Poconos?" It takes massive restraint to keep from tearing into him.

"Yeah. Reception is shit or I would've called sooner. Sorry." He clears his throat. "You got the financials squared away then, I see."

"No thanks to you." I tap my pen against the table.

"Has Kennedy responded since you uploaded the documents he requested?"

"No. I anticipate hearing something today, though. We're still shooting for closing in May. Hopefully, the citywide lockdown will be lifted by then."

"I don't know. This shit isn't blowing over. Restrictions here aren't as strict, but New York isn't fucking around. It's damn near impossible to get into the city."

"You know I don't watch the news. What little I've seen only solidifies my belief they don't know anything." I pinch the bridge of my nose. "Are you going to try to come back into the city?"

"I don't know." Evan's voice softens. "How are you holding up?"

I slump back in the chair, a bit stunned by the question. I'm falling the fuck apart. Caged and muzzled, I pace the floor, wracking my brain for things to keep me distracted because the one thing I had that kept me sane, I chased away. "I'm fine."

"Bullshit." Evan sees through it. Of course he does. We've been friends since the eighth grade. "You don't have to put on an act for me, Ben. What's going on?"

"Shit." I walk the length of the apartment. "I fucked up."

"The merger?" Evan sounds surprised. "I don't think so. You did exactly what I would have done. If this ends up putting the deal off the table, then something better will come along. You can't put it all on your shoulders."

"No." I shake my head. "I met someone."

The line is silent. Did we get disconnected?

"Evan?"

"Yeah, I'm here. I just…I think I misheard you. Did you say you met someone? Dude, the city's on lockdown. How the hell did you meet someone?"

"It's a long story."

"I've got time."

I smile at Evan's persistence. He's a fucking saint for putting up with my surly ass all these years. "You know the brownstone next to my building?"

"Yeah."

"She lives there. I saw her on the roof, planting a garden." I launch into the story, and with every passing moment, I feel the shadows around my conscience lift. For the most part, Evan's silent, interjecting every so often with a question to clarify.

When I get to the night we delivered the masks, Evan can't seem to contain his surprise. "Wait, you convinced her to break lockdown to go to the office?"

"No, she, well, she had a plan. The office is near the hospital where her friend works. We stopped at the office before taking the masks to the hospital."

"Uh-huh. Continue."

I skim over the events at the hospital and our return to the apartment. Evan bursts into laughter when I tell him our first kiss was interrupted by a cop, who happened to be her best friend's brother.

"You just can't catch a break, can you?" Evan asks between bursts of laughter.

"I'm gonna stop there." I frown, knowing I'll catch hell for what happens next, and my ego already stings, bristling at the sound of Evan's laughter.

"Oh, come on." Evan's amusement disintegrates. "Don't leave me hanging. Please tell me she left you with the worst case of blue balls after that."

"No."

"No, she didn't? Or no, you're not going to tell me?"

I contemplate hanging up, just to leave him wondering what happened next. Would serve him right after he left me to deal with all this shit by myself. I sigh.

"You're killin' me, Ben. C'mon."

"She spent the night."

"I knew it!"

I bite my tongue, knowing he wants more information, but I can't tell him. The truth feels too overwhelming, and if I put a voice to it, then it's out there. What the hell do I do with it then?

"Is that seriously all you're going to tell me?"

"Have I ever gone into details about my sex life with you?"

"Once upon a time, yes, Ben, you told me everything. But now that I think about it, you never had much of a sex life to begin with. I figured it was pointless to ask if you were getting laid."

I refuse to dignify that with a response. My teeth grind.

"Fine. Okay. No details." Evan concedes. "What

happened afterward?"

"What do you mean?"

"Ben. We've been friends longer than I care to admit, so I'm saying this from experience, but being friends with you is like trying to hug a cactus."

I stop pacing when Evan's words finally penetrate the dense fog around my brain. My whole body tenses and the overwhelming urge to throw something replaces the shock of his honesty.

"We're friends and partners. I've learned to navigate your moods. I can take it." He sighs when I don't reply. "Listen, from what you've said, this girl sounds special. I've never heard you talk about anyone the way you talk about her."

"So?"

"So, why are you talking about her in the past tense, like she's out of the picture for good?"

I hate that Evan's so fucking observant. It's served our company well, but it's shit for our friendship. "She is."

"Why? And please, spare me the bullshit excuses."

"Because I'm shit at relationships. Is that what you want me to say?"

"No, I want you to be honest with yourself." His tone softens when he continues. "You've never let yourself get close to anyone. You block everyone out. Hell, you even try to block me out, but I'm used to your shit."

"It's easier being alone."

"Of course, it seems that way. How's that working for you during this lockdown? Huh? Even a workaholic can only do so much from home."

I bite back the retort choking me because he's right. I hate that he's right. Being alone these past few weeks has cut away the self-delusion that I have my shit together. The only thing that saved me from a meltdown was Penelope.

"She was a distraction." The words are more for me than Evan.

"Was she a distraction? Or is she more than that?"

"Goddamn it, Evan. No one asked you to psychoanalyze me."

"Someone has to call you on your bullshit." He exhales with exasperation. "Listen, I don't know what you did, and I don't need to know the details, but if you let this girl go, then you're a fucking idiot."

"Tell me how you really feel." I can't control the defensive sarcasm wired in my brain.

"I did, and I'll do it again if you don't get your head out of your ass."

He's right. "Damn you."

"Hah, you'll thank me later. Now, go call her. Apologize for whatever stupid-ass thing you said and let her love you."

I scoff. "Who said anything about love?"

"You're in denial." Evan laughs. "I'll text you later. Go. Call her."

Once I end the call, I stare at the screen. Should I text her? I cross to the window and glance over at her rooftop. She's not there. Big surprise.

I set the phone aside. I don't know what to say. How do I apologize for what I did? I run both hands through my hair and pull until my scalp stings.

Nervous energy courses through me. I need to burn it. Damn. Maybe I should put the treadmill together and run. Then I'll text her. Later.

Evan's right. I'm a fucking mess, and no one wants to hug a goddamn cactus.

PENELOPE

LOCKDOWN DAY 23

"Holy shit, you're alive?" Sarcasm drips from Lucy's brusque greeting when I answer the phone.

I wince and pull the phone away from my ear an inch or

two. "Sorry. I wasn't in the mood to chat."

"Little Miss Sunshine and Lollipops doesn't feel like chatting?"

"I needed some time to think. Okay?" I sigh. "And I'm not Miss Sunshine and Lollipops. I have bad days too, you know."

"My bad. I take it back." Lucy pauses. "Did it help?"

"What?" I curl up on the couch under my favorite afghan.

"Your quiet time to think?"

"No."

"Well, I've got a few hours until my shift starts. What happened with Ben?"

"I don't know, Lucy. One minute I thought we were having a moment, and the next, he shuts me out." I shrug. "He doesn't want me." Emotions claw at the back of my throat, and tears sting my eyes. Angrily, I swipe them away.

"Whoa. Back that shit up right now. Take a breath." Lucy inhales deeply.

I imitate her and clutch the blanket tighter to my chest. Grounded again, I take another breath.

"Good. Now, pick up from where my brother caught you two making out in the park."

I smile and shake my head. Of course, Lucy wants every dirty detail. "He took me to his apartment. We had sex. Multiple times." I mutter the last part under my breath, but Lucy hears it anyway.

"Yeah, get some, girl." She clears her throat. "How was it?"

"Amazing." That word doesn't accurately describe even a fraction of the whole experience. But there aren't words to describe the sizzle and pop between Ben and me. As a physical person, I don't think too much of casual touch and personal space. But the lack of it during lockdown has left me bereft. The connection with Ben sent it into overdrive. I crave his touch so much that I physically ache for him. But how do I explain this to anyone?

"Then what's the problem. What happened?"

"The next morning, we had sex. I mean, soul scorching." I bite my lip at the memory and then the pain hits. "Afterwards, he pulled away. I mean he shut me out completely. Wouldn't talk. Nothing."

Lucy goes silent on the other end, and I wonder if I said something stupid.

"So, you two got it on multiple times, spent the night together, and then he went all moody on you?" Lucy's question sounds more like a statement. "Hmmm."

"What? Hmmm, what?" Confusion swirls around my mind, and I start to ramble. "This whole thing happened fast. I mean, we've only known each other for a few weeks. We met that night, for the first time in person. Maybe it was a bad idea. I shouldn't have…"

"Penelope! Stop. Stop. Girl. Take a breath. You're gonna drive yourself crazy."

I take several breaths, but my brain is spinning ninety miles per hour. I close my eyes. Ben's face fills the dark void in my imagination. Shit. "But I ruined it."

Lucy snorts. "No, you didn't ruin it. He did. This is Ben's issue, not yours."

"I shouldn't have jumped into bed with him."

"When was the last time you jumped into bed with anyone?"

I think for a moment and realize it's been a while. "A few years."

"And how long did you date them before you jumped in the sack?"

"A few months."

"Exactly."

"I don't understand what you're trying to say." I frown.

Lucy tuts her disappointment. "You are not an impulsive person. You don't do one-night stands. You don't do casual sex." Her voice softens. "You follow your heart, and that's not a bad thing."

"My heart lied to me." The tears spring up again, and this

time I let them fall.

"Did it?" Lucy sighs. "Listen. Lockdown has us all going a bit stir crazy. It's affecting all of us in different ways."

"So, you think the lockdown made me do something stupid?"

"It wasn't stupid, and the lockdown has nothing to do with your decision to sleep with Ben." She shifts the phone, and I hear the distinctive click of a bottle opening.

"Are you drinking?"

"One beer. Don't judge me. I work second shift."

I laugh. "No reason to get defensive."

"I'm not..." Lucy stops and then groans. "Holy shit. That makes sense."

"What makes sense?" I'm confused again, but it doesn't take much right now.

"Ben's reaction." Lucy's excitement bubbles through the phone. "Okay. This may sound crazy. But I think Ben's scared. No, he's terrified."

"Terrified? Of what?" This doesn't make sense.

"You."

"Me?" I shake my head furiously. "What the hell does that mean?"

"Sorry, I mean he's terrified of what you make him feel. Trust me, I come from a whole family of commitment-phobes, who run at the first sign of emotion." Lucy gives a self-deprecating laugh. "I would know. I won't keep a man long enough to find out if there's any future there."

A flash of realization illuminates the shadows hanging over me. Hope unfurls in my heart. "Do you think he still wants me?"

"Want you?" Lucy laughs. "Girl, I'd put a hundred bucks down that he loves you, and that scares the shit out of him."

I'm absorbing this when my phone beeps. I pull it away from my ear and check the alert. Message from Ben.

"Speak of the devil." I put Lucy on speakerphone. "Ben just texted me." I open it.

Hey. Can we talk?

"What does it say?" Lucy's excitement is contagious.

"He wants to talk." I stare at the message, and my stomach twists in knots.

"Good. Maybe he's come to his senses. I'll let you call him. You can text me later."

"Wait!" I wince at the desperation in my voice. "What do I say?"

"You'll know once you call him. See what he has to say before you apologize to him for no reason."

"And then?"

I can hear the smile in her voice. "Then follow your heart." She says goodbye and hangs up before I can even respond.

My hands shake as I respond to Ben's text. *Give me a minute.*

Call when you're ready.

The conversation with Lucy is fresh in my mind. Was I making it more complicated than it was? I chew on my fingernail and replay that morning in my mind. We had a connection. I exhale sharply. A stronger connection than I've ever felt with anyone before. In the moment, it exhilarated me, but I can see how it could be terrifying for someone who isn't used to close relationships. I can't believe Lucy saw it.

I spin the phone between my fingers. Just call him.

My heart races at the thought of his voice. I'm pretty sure it'll stop completely, once I hear it. Oh, stop. Seriously. It's nerves. Call him. What's the worst that can happen?

Without further thought, I open the phone and press the call button beside his name.

"Hey." His voice is soft and deep. He sounds relieved.

"Hi, Ben." I maintain whatever cool indifference I can muster and fail miserably. I missed him.

"I owe you an apology for the other morning." His words seem heartfelt, and I can hear how difficult it is for him to find the right ones. "And for not reaching out until now."

"I get it. You needed time." My heart aches.

"No. I mean, yes. I needed time, but I was an asshole."

"Yeah, you were." If we're being honest here then I'm going to be honest. It hurt like hell, and he needs to know it. "I really enjoyed my time with you, Ben."

"So did I."

"I'm not the type of person who jumps into bed with someone they just met." I close my eyes and push through. "What we shared wasn't just a fling to scratch an itch or whatever. I like you. A lot."

He pauses. It's the most painful silence I've ever experienced.

"Ben?"

"Fuck." The word sends a pang of need straight through me. "I'm horrible at this stuff." He exhales, and it's almost a growl.

"What stuff?"

"Relationships." Ben sounds resigned. "Penelope, I don't think I've ever been in an actual relationship in my life. Even my business partner tells me it's my weakest point, and he's known me since eighth grade."

I blink at the confession. I was not expecting any of this, but I soak it up like a thirsty sponge.

"When you, we…shit, I suck at this." He clears his throat. "I've slept like shit every night since you walked out the door. I'm trapped in my apartment and see you everywhere, which is stupid since you spent less than twelve hours here. But the time you were here, you branded everything. Even me."

My breath catches in my chest. "What are you saying, Ben?"

"Penelope. I fucked up. I pushed you away because I didn't know what to do."

"And now you know?"

"Yes." He groans, and my body heats. "I want you in my life, Penelope. Please."

"I'm still waiting for the apology part of this conversation." I ignore the way his confession sends my heartbeat into a gallop. If he wants me, he needs to work for it.

"I'm sorry for pushing you away. Please, forgive me for being the biggest asshole in New York City."

"That's quite a list to top." I pretend to ponder his apology for a moment before relenting. "But I forgive you."

"Thank you." Relief floods his voice, only to be replaced by heat. "Penelope."

My racing heart stumbles at the sinful way he says my name. "Yes, Ben."

"Shit." He pauses for a moment.

I writhe on the couch, needing him to continue whatever train of thought he highjacked.

"Sorry, Penelope. I have to take care of some business. Can I call you later?"

"Yeah, sure." I stomp on the disappointment rising to the surface.

"And Penelope." His husky voice purrs in my ear. "You'd better be naked when I call."

Oh shit. "O-okay."

He says goodbye and disconnects the call. I'm too stunned to move. Holy hell, is it a hundred degrees in the house? I throw off the afghan and fan myself with the gardening magazine sitting on the coffee table.

While that whole thing was unexpected, it wasn't unwelcome. I can't help but wonder what he has in store for me later. Naked. Oh god, I can only imagine.

Mid-fantasy, my phone pings. I smile and unlock it, expecting a text from Ben.

It's from Mr. Donovan's number. I toss the magazine, and Ben's teasing promises, aside. I forgot his test results were supposed to come today. My elation melts into concern, and it sours in the pit of my stomach.

"Oh, no." I unlock the phone to read the text from Mr. Donovan. Please, don't let it be positive.

CHAPTER THIRTEEN
DOUBLE DOWN

BEN

LOCKDOWN DAY 24

The alarm clock reads ten-thirty p.m. Exhaustion creeps in, but I know if I try to sleep, it'll just evade me the way it has for the past week. I reach for my phone. Should I text Penelope? Is she still awake?

After our conversation earlier, I'm confident we're on the same page. Apologizing has never been easy for me. But I was wrong. I'm still pissed Evan called me out on it, but, deep down, I'm thankful he did. Shit, he's going to hold that over my head until the day one of us dies.

I set the phone aside and stretch. Once I gather the papers scattered across the bed, I stack them on the nightstand. Mr. Kennedy's message this afternoon sounded promising.

He called a video conference for eleven tomorrow morning to discuss the details of the merger. I sent a message to Evan. He needs to be part of the conference. I might have stepped up to lead the process, but we're a team. I can't do this without him. Legally or metaphorically.

I set my notebook with the outlined talking points on top of the stack of papers. Once we get this deal approved, the company can finally expand. Even though I won't be leading the company, I will have more time to work on the ideas we brainstormed last fall.

Between this and finding Penelope, I finally see the blue skies breaking through the clouds above me.

I shut off the overhead light, leaving the dim lamp on. With a yawn, I sprawl out on the bed.

The phone pings. I grab it and open my messages.

Are you awake?

Yeah. I was thinking about you.

blushing emoji

I laugh and the tension eases. *What's up?*

I wanted to let you know. My neighbor's test came back. Negative.

Another surge of relief washes over me. I wasn't worried about the virus, personally, but according to Penelope, Mr. Donovan's health can't handle the onslaught of another illness. *I'm glad. Is he doing better?*

Yeah. His daughter and wife are taking good care of him.

Good. I stare at the screen. Should I tell her I miss her? God, I'm an idiot. I hold off on my reply when I see the three dots appear.

Ben.

Yes, Penelope.

I'm naked.

Well, now. I sit up and shift, propping myself against the pillows.

Isn't that what you told me you wanted?

God, yes. I said it on a whim, wanting to get a reaction, to leave her wanting more. I grin. It must have left an impression. My cock twitches at the thought of her laying bare, thinking about me. *What I want is you naked in my bed, but this will suffice tonight.*

Tease.

You started it.

Actually you started it.

Doesn't matter. I'm going to finish it. My heart's racing like I just ran ten miles. I pull down my sweatpants and take myself in hand. *Are you thinking about me?*

Yes.

Good. I want you to touch yourself. Tell me what you're doing.

My phone rings, and I damn near jump three feet off the bed. I answer the video call request. Penelope's face fills the screen. She's fucking gorgeous with her dark hair spread beneath her head. Her smile sends a pulse of longing through me.

"Hey." I hold the phone in one hand, while the other strokes my cock.

"Hi." She shifts, and I catch a glimpse of her bare shoulder. "It's hard to text and touch at the same time."

She's not wrong. I admire her bold decision. I fucking love it. Now I can see her come apart at my request. I groan.

"Are you…"

"Yeah."

"You?"

She moves, and pink blossoms across her cheeks as a moan spills from her lips. "Yeah."

"I wish you were here. I didn't get to taste you the other night."

"Oh, god."

"Do you want me to taste you, Penelope?" I lick my lips and quicken my strokes. "I'll lick that sweet little pussy until you beg me to come."

"Yes, Ben. Please. Make me come." She bites her lip, and I know she's close when her panting breaths shudder.

"That's it, baby. Just imagine my head buried between your thighs."

"Shit. Ben." The phone shakes as she falls apart. Her moans rip my release free.

I groan as the warmth coats my hand. Not enough. Never enough.

Penelope giggles.

"What?" I rise from the bed and take the phone with me into the bathroom to grab a washcloth.

"It's just." She bites her lip. "Well, that's the first time I've ever done that."

"What? Touch yourself?"

"No. I mean, yes, on a video call." The blush in her cheeks darkens. "Can I tell you a secret?"

"Of course."

"I've touched myself every night thinking about you."

And just like that, my cock jumps to attention, ready for another round. "Damn it, Penelope. You have no idea what you do to me when you say shit like that."

"I have a good idea." She laughs.

"You're evil." I shake my head. "Do you enjoy this torture?"

"Absolutely." She cocks her head, eyes sparkling. "Maybe I'll just come over and torture you in person."

I shake my head. "As much as I want that, I have a big meeting tomorrow morning. No late night for me."

She pouts, and I want to jump through the screen and kiss her senseless.

"If I get my hands on you, neither of us is going to get any fucking sleep. Not for a week at least." I immediately banish the images that conjure in my mind.

"Fine." She tilts the screen, and my mouth goes dry. Her breasts fill the screen, and the bare length of her lies beyond.

My cock jumps. Damn it. "Tease."

"Just wanted you to see what you're missing."

"You don't have to remind me." I strengthen my resolve. "This meeting needs to go off without a hitch. Once this merger is finalized, I'll make it up to you. I promise."

"Okay." She blows a kiss into the camera. "Get some sleep. Text me tomorrow."

"Goodnight, sunshine." I hang up the call.

The next morning, I'm up at six a.m. My conversation, and I use that word loosely, with Penelope led to my best night's sleep in days. I pull on my running gear and lace up my sneakers.

Thirty minutes on the treadmill leaves me drenched and panting. It feels fucking incredible.

After a long, hot shower, I shave and fix my unruly, overgrown hair. It's not perfect, but it'll work. I sit down with some scrambled eggs and coffee while I scroll through my inbox. God, I needed the routine. More than three weeks into this disruptive lockdown and I finally found my footing.

Two hours later, I change into my dark blue suit with the red pinstripe tie. I log into my VidBoom account and wait for Evan to log in. We need to discuss a few things before we move to the meeting organized by Mr. Kennedy and his colleagues.

"Hey." Evan looks like a fucking mountain man stuffed into a suit.

"What the hell? Did they sell out of razors as well as toilet paper?" I shake my head. Am I the only one taking this seriously?

"Fuck you." He rubs his hand over his beard. "I happen to like the beard. It stays."

I sigh. "You could have at least trimmed it, you know."

"No clippers." He claps his hands. "Anyway, you're looking shiny as a bright new penny. Except for that mop on your head. Geezus, is that your hair or a mutt you picked up on the streets?"

"Shut up. None of the barbers are open. At least I made an attempt today." I clear my throat. "Anyway, focus. Let's go through these notes before the meeting."

A half-hour later, Evan and I are on the same page. Confidence bolsters my mood. I disconnect the call and log into the meeting with Mr. Kennedy, using the ID and passcode his assistant emailed me yesterday.

Eleven o'clock on the money, Mr. Kennedy logs into the meeting, followed by three of his associates, his lawyer, secretary, and another man I don't recognize. Evan joins the meeting, and I sigh in relief. At least I'm not alone today. I take a deep breath.

"Ladies and gentlemen, thank you for joining me today." Mr. Kennedy smooths his hand over his yellow tie. His grey hair and neat mustache complement the dark pinstripe suit. He emanates power and poise. I'd be intimidated if I wasn't so damn inspired. I tamp down my admiration and nod.

"Good morning, sir."

"Let's get right to it, shall we?" He clears his throat and meets my gaze through the camera. "We're here to discuss the merger of Empire Industries and Solus Incorporated." He pauses to glance at the document in his hand. "I've reviewed the acquisition packet provided by Solus Incorporated. I will admit, I'm impressed."

"Thank you, Mr. Kennedy." I acknowledge the compliment on behalf of both Evan and myself.

He inclines his head. "Mr. Statler and Mr. Waldorf started this company with very little capital in a small Jersey warehouse. Within ten years, it's become one of the most important suppliers on the Eastern seaboard. Bravo, gentlemen."

Pride surges through my veins. Finally, someone sees the potential.

Mr. Kennedy leans forward, his eyes clear and focused. "After reviewing the financials with my accounting department, I've made a decision that will benefit both of us in the long term."

I stare at the screen in confusion. "Sir?"

"The pandemic and subsequent lockdowns have put a strain on the global economy. It has hit the American economy hard, and businesses across the country are feeling the impact." He pauses. "Empire Industries is not immune, and neither is Solus Incorporated."

"What are you saying, Mr. Kennedy?" I can barely form the words past the fear, rising like bile in my throat.

"I propose we postpone the merger for a year. This will give the economy a chance to stabilize and businesses an opportunity to reorganize in the wake of this financial turmoil."

The thoughts in my head spin like a tornado, and I can't grasp any of them to articulate even a basic acknowledgment.

"After a year, we will revisit the details of the merger and proceed forward, if all parties are amenable." He focuses his attention on me. "Does this meet your approval, Mr. Statler?"

What the hell am I supposed to say? Thanks for fucking nothing?! Rage spirals inside me, but I slam a lid on it and smile. "If you believe this is the right course of action, sir, then, of course."

"Very well." Mr. Kennedy leans back in his chair. "Thank you all for your hard work and dedication. We'll make it through this and be all the stronger for it. Have a good day, everyone."

A flurry of hasty goodbyes filters through as everyone logs off. I disconnect the call and stare at the blank screen. What the fuck just happened? Everything I busted my ass for, gone. Poof. Over. Thanks a lot, global pandemic, for fucking us all over. I can't help but take the whole thing personally.

The phone rings. It's Evan. I ignore it and push away from the table. In a daze, I wander into the kitchen, pulling my tie free. Fuck it.

Nothing matters. All that work for what? A backhanded compliment and try again next year.

I grab the bottle of scotch in the cabinet. I don't even bother with a glass and tip the liquid down my throat. It burns, but I don't care. The whole world is burning. I might as well go down in flames with it.

PENELOPE

LOCKDOWN DAY 24

For the twentieth time today, I pick up my phone and open Ben's messages. I've typed something at least a dozen times before deleting it and setting the phone aside. The timer on the stove dings. I pull the fresh blueberry muffins from the oven and set them to cool on the stovetop.

It's after two o'clock. His meeting was at eleven. He told me he'd text afterward. But still nothing. I fidget with the phone for a few moments before abandoning it completely.

I plop down at the table and pull the laptop closer. As I scroll through the color wheel on the Sherwin Williams website, I debate what colors to use in the kitchen and living room. The house doesn't need a full remodel, but it could do with a fresh coat of paint and a few minor updates. Lucy was right. I need to put my own creative touch on the space.

Grandpa maintained everything with meticulous care, but he didn't have an eye for décor. Grandma was more interested in her gardens and sewing than anything else. They asked Mr. Donovan to take over maintenance for the building a few years ago at Grandma's insistence. She was tired of hearing Grandpa complain about how much work it was. God, I miss them.

Finally, I settle on an eggshell cream color for the kitchen. The dark cabinetry needs a lighter color. My attention drifts to the blueberry goodness cooling on the rack.

The muffins call to me. I make a note to take some to the Donovans. Maybe I should take some to Ben too.

Wait. Does he even like blueberry muffins?

This time I don't hesitate. I send him a text. *I know you're busy. Just want to know how you feel about blueberry muffins.*

Five minutes pass. No reply. I send another message.

*Ben, can I bring you some muffins? *Winking Emoji**

I cringe. That was corny. I mean, I meant it both ways, but seeing it now, yikes.

Another five minutes pass.

You okay?

Now I'm worried. After last night, I thought we were on the same page. I thought he wanted me. But why isn't he answering? Something is wrong.

"Screw it." I change into a pair of jeans and a sweater before slipping on my shoes. I check my reflection in the mirror to make sure I don't look like a train wreck. My hair is tousled but easily tamed with a pony tail. Makeup? I shake my head and throw some things in an overnight bag. Getting all dolled up has never been my thing. Besides, Ben saw me without anything on last night, and I didn't hear any complaints.

Heat curls through me. I want to wrap myself around him and never come up for air. I've been thinking about his promise to bury his face between my thighs. I stumble when I walk into the kitchen. He's got me so distracted, I can't even walk.

I divide the muffins into two bags and tuck my purse into my overnight bag. I sling it over my shoulder and slip from the house. Plants should be good. The oven is off. I mentally check the list as I walk down the stairs.

Outside the Donovans' door, I set the bag of muffins. Then I put my mask on and slip out onto the sidewalk. There aren't a lot of people outside. I pass one couple between my building and Ben's. I pop in the door, and the attendant eyes me suspiciously.

"Can I help you?" I can barely hear him through the mask.

I lift the bag of muffins. "Delivery, seventh floor, apartment fourteen."

He nods and presses the button to unlock the door.

"Have a great day!" I chirp before heading to the elevator.

Once I reach the seventh floor, my heart won't stop beating against my ribs. I knock on apartment number fourteen.

"Ben. It's Penelope." I persist pounding on the door. He's home. He has to be. The city's still on lockdown, he can't be anywhere else. Right? "Ben!" I bang harder.

"I swear, I'll call the cops to do a welfare check if you don't answer this door!" I can't help but throw Lucy's threat in for good measure.

I stop when I hear the deadbolt slide and the clink of the chain against it. I don't know what I was expecting when Ben opened the door, but it sure as hell wasn't this.

He looks like his last fuck just took a nose dive off the Brooklyn Bridge. A red pinstripe tie hangs limp around the collar of his unbuttoned shirt. His blue trousers have a dark stain on the thigh. He grips the bottle in his hand tighter.

"What are you doing here?" His voice sways toward the end of his question.

I step closer and the overpowering smell of scotch hits me. I put my hand on his chest and push him back. He refuses to budge.

"Are you going to let me in?" I search his gaze for some kind of explanation.

He remains immovable. A brick wall.

I sigh. "Please, let me in. I brought you muffins." I hold up the bag.

"Go home, Penelope." The muscle in his jaw flexes.

"Not until you tell me what the hell happened."

"I don't want you here."

"Liar."

We face-off, and I won't lie, under normal circumstances this kind of power play would turn me on. But holding his gaze, I see it. The flash of hurt and disappointment deep in his brown eyes. Damn it. I can't leave him like this.

A few tense moments stretch between us. Finally, he concedes and steps aside.

Inside, it looks like a hurricane blew through his apartment. Papers lay scattered everywhere. The once tidy apartment resembles a disaster area.

I set my bag down on the floor and put the muffins on the kitchen counter. When I turn to face Ben, he's propped against the wall, nursing the bottle in his hand.

"Okay, that's enough of that." I snatch the bottle from his hand and pour what remains down the sink.

"Hey!" He lunges forward to grab it and trips, nearly falling into the refrigerator. He grips the counter and steadies himself.

I toss the empty bottle in the trash and round on him. "You're shitfaced already. Any more and you'll cause permanent damage, aside from pickling yourself." I prop my hands on my hips when he straightens to his full height and glares down at me.

"I didn't ask you to come here. And don't you dare treat me like a child."

"Then don't act like one."

"Why are you here? Can't you take a hint?"

"So, you were ignoring my texts."

He drops his gaze and leans against the wall.

I step closer and put my hand on his shoulder. "Come on. You need to lay down."

"Don't coddle me." He jerks his arm away and stumbles toward the bedroom.

I sigh. There's no use arguing with him when he's in this state. I've dealt with enough drunks to read between the lines. My roommates in college were notorious party animals, and I was always the responsible one. It seems I still am. I follow him down the hall. He collapses on the unmade bed.

I kneel and pull his shoes off. He lays with one arm draped over his eyes. I wrangle the shirt from his belligerent person.

"Stubborn as a mule," I mumble under my breath as I pull his pants off. He's wearing nothing but socks and boxer briefs. I suck in a breath at the sight of his sculpted torso and long, muscular limbs. Damn it, stop lusting over an intoxicated man.

He hasn't opened his eyes since his head hit the pillow. I shake my head. Did he drink that whole bottle? I pull the blanket up to cover him.

There, now I'm not distracted by all that skin. I take a deep breath. Nestled beneath the white blanket with his dark hair splayed around his face, I'm struck by how vulnerable he looks. And how sexy. Shit. Okay, tidy up.

I focus my energy on cleaning the apartment. I'm not sure what happened, but I have a feeling it wasn't anything good to make him trash the place. I pick up the papers and notice his phone lying in the corner of the room under the kitchen chair.

It vibrates, flashing the caller ID across the screen. *Evan.* I answer it.

"Hello, this is Ben's phone."

"Oh, thank god, someone answered. Who is this? Is Ben there? Is he okay? Oh shit, this isn't a nurse or a cop, is it?"

More muttered swearing filters through the phone.

"No, no. I'm not a cop or a nurse. I'm a friend of Ben's. He's...uh, taking a nap."

"A nap?" The man on the other end pauses, as if pondering the truth of those words. "Ben never takes naps. He hates naps. Who is this again?"

"Penelope. I'm a friend of Ben's."

The man scoffs. "Ben doesn't have any of those. Wait...oh shit. You're...Oh...OHHHHHH."

"I'm sorry, who are you again?" I'm intrigued and confused by this whole interaction.

"Evan Waldorf." He clears his throat. "I'm Ben's partner at Solus Industries and his best friend."

"Really?"

"Yes."

"How long have you known Ben?" I set the papers on the table and continue to collect them as we talk.

"Years. We met in Mr. Mushrush's eighth grade English class."

"That's a long time." I sit at the dining table.

"You have no idea." Evan chuckles. "Listen, I've been trying to call Ben for the past three hours."

"Oh, he's ignoring you too?"

"Yeah. Well, after the news we got this morning, I understand why he wants some time alone. He's worked so hard on this merger, making sure everything lined up perfectly."

"Oh no. What happened?" That explains why he pushed me away again and the scotch.

"Wait, if he's ignoring both of us, how are you answering his phone? Are you at his place?" Evan sounds surprised and curious.

"He never texted me after his meeting. So I decided to bring him some muffins." It sounds innocent enough, but even I hear the sexy implication of my confession.

"Muffins. Uh-huh. Well, where is he now?"

"Asleep."

"Seriously?"

"Yes."

"Was this after the muffins?"

I almost choke at the question. Cheeky bastard. "For the record, he was drunk when I showed up. Demolished a whole bottle of scotch. I told him to go sleep it off."

"Shit. I'm sorry. I shouldn't have implied...well, after he told me he was seeing someone, I guess I assumed." He sighs. "That's what assuming gets me. My apologies, Penelope. Thank you for checking on him."

"I knew something was wrong when he ignored my texts." I toy with the edge of the papers. "I'm glad I checked on him."

"I'm glad you did too. I'm not in the city. Otherwise, I would have come myself."

"You going to tell me what happened at the meeting this morning?"

"I think it would be best if Ben told you himself."

I knew he would say that. "I'll let him know you called."

"Thanks, Penelope. You're a saint, you know that. You'd have to be to put up with Ben's shit."

"I'm in good company then."

"I see what you did there. I like you. Keep an eye on him."

"Of course. Later."

The phone's nearly dead. I take it to the bedroom and plug it in.

I pull the curtains closed and shut the door, leaving Ben to sleep it off. Well, since I'm here, I might as well make myself at home. I'm not going anywhere until he tells me what happened today.

Determined, I raid the fridge and see what I can whip up for dinner. I'm starving.

CHAPTER FOURTEEN
AMENDS

BEN

LOCKDOWN DAY 25

Who's singing? I crack my eyes and wince. Even the small amount of sunlight peeking through the curtains sends pain shooting through my head. Oh, god. My mouth is dry and gritty. I vaguely remember Evan joking about the hungover-shit-in-the-mouth taste. I'm not sure how he came to that conclusion, but right now, it's the closest thing to an accurate description I can imagine.

Soft strains of music filter through the closed bedroom door. A rush of broken images flashes through my head. Penelope. Muffins. I slowly sit up and the blanket falls away.

I run my hand across my bare chest. What the hell happened? The meeting. The merger. Shit. I flop back onto the bed and pull the blanket over my thundering head.

"Oh, you're alive." Penelope's angelic voice does nothing to soothe the stabbing pain.

Play dead. Maybe if I don't move, she'll go away. I can't deal with this right now. The blanket whooshes as it's ripped off the bed. I groan.

"Come on. Go take a shower, brush your teeth, and pop some Advil. I'm making breakfast."

I glare at her.

"Don't look at me like I just shit in your Cheerios." She puts her hands on her hips. "You did this to yourself." Our gazes lock and I'm struck by how cute she is when she's doling out instructions like a drill sergeant. "Go." She points toward the bathroom before retreating to the kitchen.

After a few moments to catch my breath, I pull myself up to my feet and drag myself to the bathroom. The shower revives what few brain cells remain, and my mouth no longer tastes like it was used as a public toilet. I throw on a pair of sweats and a t-shirt before grabbing 800 mg of ibuprofen.

I stagger into the kitchen. My papers are stacked neatly on the buffet beside my laptop. The delightful scent of coffee and bacon lingers in the air. My stomach growls. I sit at the table where she's placed a plate of eggs, bacon, and a blueberry muffin. I eagerly take the coffee mug from her hand and sip it. It's fucking heaven.

When I look up, her expression stuns me. She's smiling but I can see she's keeping a guarded distance. Shit. I don't remember much. The fury of disappointment unleashes inside me once more. I only remember the meeting. All that hard work. Wasted.

"Eat." She sits across the table and picks up her fork.

I pop the pills and wash them down with coffee before taking a few tentative bites. Slowly, the twisting pain in my head eases. We eat in silence for a few minutes. I shake my head and scoff.

"Don't like the food?" She takes a sip of her coffee.

"No, it's good." I clear my throat. "It's just, well, I think this is the first meal we've had together."

"Yeah. You're right." She pushes the eggs around with her fork. "It's nice though."

I nod and take a few bites before I work up enough courage to ask the questions burning a hole in my brain. "I think I owe you another apology."

Her fork clatters against the plate. She quickly picks it up and stares at me like I've sprouted a second head. "Wow. Two in one week. Is this some kind of record?"

The sass is strong with this one. I like it. "That's a bold assessment. We've only known each other for a few weeks."

"I'm a quick study." She cocks her head and watches me. "Evan elevated me to sainthood for putting up with your shit."

"What?" I nearly choke on a mouthful of scrambled eggs. After washing them down with coffee, I catch my breath. "You spoke to Evan? When?"

"Yesterday."

"Shit." My head spins. "Okay. Let's start at the beginning. How did you get here?"

Penelope finishes her food, pushing the plate aside before responding. She leans on the table with the coffee mug cradled between her hands. "I walked."

I could kiss the smirk off her lips. "Yes, I figured that much."

"I texted you." She taps the cup. "You didn't reply. So, I brought you muffins." Her gaze drops to the table. "I was worried about you."

My heart clenches. Shit. "Penelope."

She holds her hand up. "I brought muffins to surprise you, but when I got here, you were already trashed. And so was your apartment." She takes a deep breath. "You told me to go home. You didn't want me."

"Fuck." I slide my hand through my hair. "I'm so sorry, Penelope. I didn't mean it."

"I know." She holds my gaze and smiles, although it doesn't quite reach her eyes. "That's why I poured your scotch down the sink and made you go to bed. You're not a pretty drunk, by the way."

I scoff. "So I've been told."

"I made myself at home and cleaned up."

"You've been here all night?"

"Yeah. I crashed on the couch." She grins. "You snore like a goddamn chainsaw when you're drunk."

I almost snort my coffee mid-sip.

She laughs.

I like this, what we have here, right now. A peaceful sort of companionship. The communication is nice too, refreshing. What I love the most is having her here with me, and her sticking around, even though she's seen me at my lowest point.

"Again. I'm sorry. I'm glad you came." I rub the back of my neck. "I'm glad you stuck around."

"Me too."

"You spoke to Evan?"

"Yeah, he called while I was cleaning, and you were dead to the world."

"I bet he was surprised."

She covers her mouth to smother a laugh. "Yeah, you could say that."

"Did he tell you what an asshole I am?"

"I didn't need him to tell me what I already know."

"Nice burn." I push the empty plate away and sigh. "I deserved that."

"You may be a gruff asshole, who's awkward as hell when it comes to relationships, but it doesn't make me like you any less. I enjoy spending time with you." Penelope takes my hand and squeezes.

The brush of her fingertips against mine sparks a heat that unfurls through me. I pull her toward me, and in the next second, she's curled on my lap. I missed this. Her touch. Her company. Her honesty.

"I love being with you." I struggle to find the right words and tighten my arms around her. "I know I suck at this whole relationship thing. But I want to give it a shot. You and me, I mean."

"Me too." She pulls back and cups my face in her hand. Her hazel eyes burn into mine. "But if we're going to do this, then I need you to talk to me. You can't shut me out."

I sigh. "You're right. I'll work on that."

"Good. You can start by telling me what the hell happened yesterday in your meeting that sent you into this downward spiral."

"The merger I've worked on for six months went up in smoke." Voicing the words sends my mood into a nosedive. I shift restlessly in my chair.

Penelope takes my face between her hands. "You're

doing it again. Don't push me away. Walk me through it."

I explain the merger and the plans moving forward. Then I recount Mr. Kennedy's decision from the meeting. "It's like the floor has been ripped out from under me."

She kisses my cheek and lays her head on my shoulder. "It's okay to be disappointed. Especially now. This pandemic and the lockdown, they've disrupted our routine, our connections with our friends and family, and our plans. It's natural to feel frustrated. Everyone's feeling it in some way."

Her touch and her words combine to soothe my agitation. "It sucks. I worked so fucking hard on this. I had plans. This lockdown, the virus, it fucked up everything." The need to retreat and lock everyone out claws at my mind. Instead, I let her ground me in the moment and breathe deep. She smells so good, like lemon, fresh air, and sunshine. My body relaxes.

"You know." She strokes my hair. "Without this lockdown, we never would have met."

The realization settles over me. "Yeah, you're right."

"I'm sorry your merger didn't go through, but it doesn't mean all your hard work has gone to waste. I'm sure Mr. Kennedy sees the dedication you have to your company." She rubs my scalp, and I groan. "He didn't close the door on the idea. He's only trying to protect his financial investment. You can't blame him for that."

"No." She's right. Of course, I know this. I knew it the moment Mr. Kennedy made the announcement. But it still hurt like hell. I should've seen it coming, and that stings more than the disappointment because I could've been better prepared for the obvious disruption the pandemic would cause.

"Everything happens for a reason."

"That's so cliché."

"It may be, but it's true." She rubs her cheek against mine. "I've got a whole bag of clichés. Want me to pull them all out?"

"God, please no."

"A friend in need is a friend indeed."

I shove her off my lap and stand up. "Seriously, I'll make you leave."

She motions to my hands on her shoulders. "Actions speak louder than words."

"Penelope. Stop. You're giving me a headache."

"Well, maybe you need a hair of the dog that bit you."

"You're ridiculous." I grab her by the waist and pull her toward the bedroom.

"Flattery will get you nowhere." She laughs hysterically when I pick her up and toss her onto the bed.

"That's it. Maybe this will shut you up." I climb onto the bed and pin her beneath me. I admire her bright eyes and flushed cheeks before I kiss her.

She melts into me. Coffee and sweet blueberry linger on her tongue. I groan and grind my hips against hers.

"I missed you," I whisper between kisses.

Her hands tangle in my hair. "I missed you too."

"I have a crazy idea."

"What's that?"

"Move in with me."

She blinks up at me. "What about my garden?"

"Good point."

"You can move in with me."

I stare at her like she's just discovered the secrets of the universe and the meaning of life. "Under one condition."

"Anything."

"No more clichés."

The wicked gleam in her eyes betrays her before she speaks, and I kiss her.

"I see you like to play dirty."

"You're going to be the death of me." I kiss her again until we're both too lost in each other to continue our battle of clichés.

A faint buzzing cuts through the haze of need. I see my phone flashing on the nightstand. Mr. Kennedy's ID splays across the screen.

"Shit. I need to take this." I climb over her, ignoring her giggles and protests. "Behave, this will only take a minute." I settle on the edge of the bed and answer the call.

"Mr. Kennedy?"

"Statler, it's about bloody time you answered. I've been trying to call since last night."

"My apologies, sir. I've been having issues with my phone." I wince at the lie, but I can't bring myself to admit my unprofessional response to the outcome of yesterday's meeting.

"I wanted to clarify something that I didn't express accurately during the meeting."

"Sir?"

"You've done a hell of a job in building and maintaining Solus Incorporated. Make no mistake, I have every intention of merging our companies, but I cannot, in good conscience, make such a risky venture while the market is at this volatile stage."

"I understand." I swallow the lump in my throat. Was he trying to make me feel worse or give me hope?

"In the interim, Empire Industries will stand beside Solus Incorporated, providing funding, if necessary, for the basic maintenance of the company should they require the support."

Surprise robs me of the ability to respond. It takes a moment for the realization seep into my hungover brain. "Thank you."

"I have no doubt Solus Incorporated will have even more to offer Empire next year when we finally merge."

"Yes, of course."

"Don't let this discourage you. I'm sure the lockdown is giving you plenty of time to brainstorm some new ideas for the company."

I glance over my shoulder at Penelope, who's now standing at the foot of the bed, peeling off her clothes at a painfully erotic pace. She grins as the first garment hits the floor.

"I have some ideas, yes."

"I'll leave you to it then."

"Thank you. Goodbye, sir." I hang up the phone and shoot across the bed, just as she kicks her pants aside.

"Am I distracting you?" She purrs as I pull her against me. Soft skin slides beneath my fingers, and I swear I've died and gone to heaven.

"You've been distracting me for weeks, woman." I growl and nip at the soft spot below her ear.

She sighs and wraps her arms around me. We collapse onto the bed in a tangle of limbs and smothered giggles. I kiss her until I can't think.

Something vibrates against my hip.

"Damn it." I pull the phone from under us and answer it. "What?"

"Um…bad time?" Evan's voice breaks through.

"Yes."

"Muffin time?"

"What?" I'm confused by the reference, but Penelope launches into a fit of giggles.

"He'll call you later, Evan. He's gotta eat his muffin." Tears spring to her eyes as the laughter veers on the point of hysterics.

"Too much information. Go. Enjoy. Bye." He hangs up.

"Finally." I toss the phone aside. "Now, what's this about eating my muffin?" I skim my hands along her stomach and over her hips, dragging her underwear down her legs.

"Yes." Her eyes drift closed. "I've been thinking about this since the other night."

"Me too, baby." When I taste her, she moans, and it's the sweetest piece of heaven.

Her fingers tangle in my hair, and suddenly, we're both lost in our own little, bliss-soaked universe, with nothing on our hands but time.

I guess lockdown does have its benefits.

Penelope

Approximately One Year Later

Classic rock reverberates off the walls. I dance around the kitchen, as I finish washing the dishes. Water splashes down my shirt and I jump back.

"Oh, man." I pull the soaked fabric between my fingers to wring it out. "That's what I get for dancing and doing the dishes at the same time."

I grab the dish towel and dab the spot, knowing it's hopeless. I'll just have to change. I finish the last of the dishes and wipe the counters. The scent of chocolate chip cookies fills the kitchen. Ben's favorite, baked especially to celebrate the finalization of the merger between Solus and Empire.

I contemplated making blueberry muffins, even though I know they're not his favorite. I remember exactly where those blueberry muffins led us. Whew, it's too warm in here.

I pull the wet shirt off and drape it over the towel rack in the bathroom. The clock beside the bed reads four-fifteen. Ben should be home by five-thirty. Plenty of time to jump in the shower and dress.

His text specifically said, "Be ready by six. Dress nice."

It's suspicious. Ben doesn't do surprises. After a year of living together, I learned this quickly. The man doesn't even like it when I invite friends over for an impromptu dinner. No. He likes to be prepared. Organized. But never boring.

No. Life with Ben is not boring. It's amazing. Deep beneath the brooding workaholic layer is a sweet, tender teddy bear. It may not be action-packed, but it's definitely an adventure. Even the few trips to visit our respective families unveiled interesting depths to the man I'm fortunate enough to call my husband.

I trace my fingers across the frame of our wedding photo taken last October. Just the two of us with a glorious sunset and the Brooklyn Bridge in the background. The weather was perfect. It seemed fitting that our wedding should be as non-traditional as our courtship.

After a quick shower, I indulge with a bit of makeup and braid my hair before pulling on my jeans and a white, lightweight cashmere sweater.

The sound of the front door closing sets my heart racing.

"Penelope?" His voice still makes me weak.

"Honey, you're home early. You said six." I round the corner and freeze when I see him.

He's not wearing the suit he had on this morning when he left the house. I take in the sight before me. Jeans, a white t-shirt, and a cardigan. He runs a hand through his hair and smiles.

I brace myself against the wall to keep from sprinting across the room and climbing him like a tree. Something's fishy. I ignore my hormones for a moment and purse my lips. "Where's your suit?"

"What?" He crosses to the kitchen, grabs a cookie from the rack, and takes a bite.

Who knew eating a chocolate chip cookie could be so damn sexy? I lick my lips. Damn him. He's distracting me. I shake my head.

"Fine. I'm ready. Where are we going?" I grab my purse from the table.

He responds with a devastating smile.

"Keep smiling like that and I swear we won't be going anywhere tonight."

Ben licks the chocolate from his thumb. "Would you rather stay here?"

I can't form a coherent response because he's covered the distance between us in a few short strides and all I can smell is him and the cookies. It's intoxicating.

He's grinning. He knows exactly what he does to me. Damn him. His breath caresses my ear. "As much as I would love to drag you into the bedroom and keep you there all night, I have something for you."

The soft kiss he leaves on my lips does nothing to sate

my hunger. "Is it better than sex?"

Ben laughs. "Probably not. Come on." He takes my hand and leads me out the door. Instead of turning to go down the stairs, he leads me the opposite way.

"Why are we going to the roof?"

A lopsided smile is his only response.

He opens the door and holds it. I step out onto the rooftop and gasp.

The setting sun disappears over the horizon, casting shadows on the rooftop. Strings of lights hang across the space, zig-zagging and glittering in the twilight. A food-laden table sits beyond the garden bed. Tears blur my vision when I see our friends' smiling faces. Lucy, her brother Joey, and Ben's partner Evan sit at the table watching us.

I turn to Ben. "What is this?"

"Dinner with our friends."

I elbow him in the side and wipe the tears away. "I can see that. What are we celebrating? Your merger?"

Ben shakes his head. "We don't need a reason." He kisses my cheek. "Every day is a celebration."

"Oh, Ben. That was just the cheesiest line ever." I bury my face against his chest. "I must be rubbing off on you."

He grasps my chin in his hand and I meet those intense whiskey eyes. "I love you, Penelope. You're the best thing that has ever happened to me. Our lockdown love affair is the stuff of ridiculous romantic comedies." He kisses me. "I wouldn't have it any other way."

"Get a room! Or I'll arrest you for public indecency." Joey's shout echoes across the roof.

"Ben, stop hogging your wife. I haven't seen her all week!" Lucy adds to the fray.

"The natives..."

Ben smacks my ass. "I warned you about using clichés in my presence."

My face heats at the soft press of his palm against my backside.

We join our friends, and I'm struck by just how far we've

come. A year ago, I never would have imagined lockdown would lead me to the love of my life. In a way, I'm glad it played out the way it did.

I hug Lucy before taking the seat beside her.

She pours me a glass of wine. "Listen, I want to apologize."

"Why?"

"I admit, I wasn't completely sold on your seventh-floor stalker and this whirlwind marriage." She winks. "But when he called me to help get this together for you, I knew you found a good one."

"I can't believe you did this behind my back." I glance around the rooftop. "This is why he told me he'd take care of the garden this week." I scowl at Ben who's deep in a heated debate with Joey and Evan over what sounds like baseball. I shake my head.

"Men."

"I'll toast to that." Lucy lifts her glass.

We sip our wine and enjoy the spring evening.

I spy Lucy over the rim of my glass. Her gaze keeps shifting to the men.

"Lucy, I know for a fact you're not looking at my husband or your brother." I chuckle and lean closer. "Are you checking out Evan?"

She drains the contents of her glass and pours another. "Psh, no."

Evan's handsome, classically so, with his dark blonde hair and piercing blue eyes. He matches Ben in height, but he's much broader with more defined muscle than the typical runner's build.

Lucy's cheeks flare a deep pink.

Evan looks our way as though sensing our conversation is about him. I smile and wave. Lucy hides behind her wine glass.

He waves back, allowing his attention to linger on Lucy for a hot second, then returns to his discussion with Ben and Joey.

"You should absolutely ask him out."

"Hell, no. I'm done with men. Besides, I told you before, I'm not a one-man kinda woman."

"C'mon, Lucy. Evan's a great guy. You two would make a cute couple." I nudge her. "It's not like you two haven't talked before."

Lucy chokes on her wine and avoids my gaze.

"Lucy?"

Her face blossoms in crimson.

"Oh my god, spill it."

"Keep your voice down." Lucy kicks me under the table when the guys look up at us in unison. They shrug and return to their conversation. Lucy lowers her voice. "We...kinda hooked up already."

"LUCY!" I clap my hand over my mouth.

"Everything okay over there?" Evan watches us with concern.

"All good. Thanks. Carry on." I round on Lucy. "When the hell did this happen? Why didn't you tell me?" I'm hurt and shocked by this development. How could I have possibly missed it?

"The Christmas party."

"My Christmas party?" I feel like I'm looking at her for the first time.

She nods. "It wasn't a big deal." Her heated glance at Evan tells a different story.

"I knew you two would make a cute couple." I grin. "How was it?"

Lucy's eyes glaze over, and I know she's already lost. "Amazing."

"Then, what's the problem?"

"Me. I'm the problem." Lucy finishes her second glass of wine and pours the third.

"Slow down there, lady." I slide the glass from her hand and set it out of reach. "Let's eat something first, then we can discuss where to go from here."

Lucy nods. "Good. I'm starving." She casts one last

longing glance in Evan's direction just as he looks up, and I'm caught between their magnetic attraction.

I glance at Ben, whose brow arches in question. I wave him off, a promise to tell him later. He nods and serves the fresh lasagna from Mario's down the street.

Ben raises his glass. "To Penelope, who deserved a better first date than texting a perfect stranger while binge-watching Tiger King during a global pandemic."

"And to Ben, who needed some sunshine in his life," Evan adds with a wink in my direction.

"Aww, you guys. I love you all." My heart nearly bursts, and I can't think of a better way to spend my post-lockdown days than surrounded by the people I love.

THE END

CRAVING MORE?

READ A HOLIDAY LOVE AFFAIR

LUCY AND EVAN'S STORY

Other Books By Kirsten S. Blacketer

<u>Craving 1985 Series</u>

When I Found You
Can't Fight This Feeling
She Gives Love a Bad Name
Owner of a Lonely Heart
Just What I Needed

<u>Historical</u>

An Irresistible Shadow
A Shadow's Kiss
Mississippi Moonshine
Deceiving the Earl
Jewel of Winter
At Winter's Demand
Under Winter's Control
Seducing Winter's Gentleman
Stealing the Widow's Heart
Seduction on the Alpine Express
Temptation on the Alpine Express

<u>Contemporary</u>

A Lockdown Love Affair
A Holiday Love Affair
Mistletoe and Mistakes
Confessions of a Fangirl
Confessions of a Gamer Girl
Confessions of a Glamour Girl
The Flight Before Christmas

<u>Fantasy/FairyTale</u>

Curse of the Huntsman's Jewel
The Huntsman's Revenge

<u>Pirates and Persuasion</u>

Queen Takes Hook

ABOUT THE AUTHOR
KIRSTEN S. BLACKETER

Kirsten S. Blacketer is a multi-published indie author of both historical and contemporary romance. When she's not writing, she homeschools her two children and enjoys time with her family. In those moments of freedom, she devours romance novels while sipping a glass of wine. Age has only shown her that writing villains can be just as fun as heroes. Her next life goals are to write a New York Times Bestseller and one day have Adam Driver play a starring role in a film version of one of her books. A girl can dream, right?

Read more at **http://kirstensblacketer.com.**

ALSO WRITES AS JEN BRADLEE